Nightmare Fuel: Four Short Stories to Ruin Your Night

Scott Gray

1

2

Reprieve

–A Two for One–

As Kristy Northram pulled up to the church, she flipped down her car's visor and checked her face. Her husband gave her hell for checking her makeup constantly, but her long brown hair had a tendency to hang over her face, smearing her makeup. But he was dead now. Both him, and her son, both in one night.

Part of her desperately craved a cigarette. The thoughts she was having as of late had a way of leading to that.

A comparable part of her wanted to never step foot into a car again. From here on out, cars would always be one of two things that made her think of the family she lost.

5

The other was alcohol. Perhaps there was a third thing, she wondered frequently for the past four days: her inability to put a stop to her husband's drinking long ago.

It was as if people knew she was thinking that, because constantly she heard "It's not your fault" as if it were on a skipping record.

"It's not your fault."

"Not your fault."

"Fault.

No, it was Deckland's fault. He could've given up drinking years ago. For good. He managed to do it a few times. even. Albeit, for a duration they both knew would last but so long. It was unspoken, but it was known. He wasn't much for wagons. She knew it subconsciously; he knew it beyond a shadow of a doubt.

Kristy rolled her eyes in the visor mirror and flipped it back up forcefully, eliciting a thump that nearly startled her. Today, just about anything would do that. She was here for Beck, in truth. Beck and Beck alone, killed by her husband's drinking…and her inability to do anything about it.

Fault.

There's a feeling we all get, when we know someone is staring daggers at us. Kristy felt that now and even knew from where as she heard gravel being pushed out of the way of tires as a blue Hyundai Sonata pulled up next to her. With glacial pace, she turned her head to see Deckland's parents, both scowling, his mother, Casey, looking right at her.

I wasn't even there, bitch. Lower your weapons' sights.

I can just imagine it now, "No, you weren't there, should've been…blech blech blech bawk bawk bawk."

She shook her head like an etch-a-sketch, looking up to see Casey and husband Craig making their way up the cobblestone walkway to the entrance of the church.

Whenever she was going to get out of the car, it certainly wasn't now. The walkway was maybe twenty feet but making her way up it with them would seem like a time loop. Instead, her mind wandered as she looked to her car's digital clock: 2:47. Thirteen minutes left…still time.

—

"Do hangovers ever get any better, Dad?" Sixteen-year-old Beck had asked not long ago after his first night of drinking at a neighborhood party close to their house. They nearly had to force him out the door to go. Beck was a shy one, and Kristy appreciated it up to a point. There's an age where it's time for the trunk to grow branches. On the other hand, at least it felt like she still had her baby. Still, while other parents complained about their kids snipping and snapping at every little word, she couldn't say the same. If anything, as Beck ventured into his teens, she found that their relationship remained thick, if not thickening.

To Beck's question, Deckland had laughed for what felt like a minute before saying, "No, they get so much worse. Or you could go the alcoholic route and never get hangovers because you're drunk all the time and end up feeling like a..."

"Deck." She snapped, controlled yet forceful. It was an abbreviation she used seldomly within their marriage.

"– Uh, basically it's lose-lose with booze," Deckland reframed and finished his answer.

"Yes," she had said with a smile to Beck.

Then, Beck ran out of the room. She could hear him stumbling and bumping on the railing as he made his way up the staircase before slamming the bathroom door shut.

—

A knock rapped on Kristy's window. It was Casey, with her perma-scowl and a now-beckoning finger with some truly odious blue artificial nails to decorate her wrinkly, aging fingers.

With a sigh and as polite a forced smile as she could muster, she exited the car and faced her mother-in-law. *Oh, the weather outside is frightful, but my mother-in-law she's sooo delightful.*

"You even want to be here, Kristy?"

No.

"I'm ready, sorry about that." She pushed the car door shut without looking and made her way up to the church's entrance, letting Casey go in first. Her mother-in-law did not hold open the door.

They made their way down the aisle and reached the

pew to the very front. There, they sat and faced two coffins.

Casey had arranged the logistics of most of this. One

of Kristy's mother-in-law's greatest disappointments was

how her son and his wife had failed to create a suitably

religious environment for their son. Kristy would have

known as much even if Casey hadn't managed to bring it up

at every holiday social event. Never organically, of course.

A young priest, whom Kristy recognized from high

school as Ray Smith but must be Priest Smith or Pastor

Smith now, approached the podium and sighed.

"When things arrive in our lives in a manner that is

fully unexpected, it is frequently quite difficult to take stock.

Quite difficult." His eyes scanned the room, moved to

Kristy, then Casey and Craig, then back to Kristy.

He continued, "We will begin with the Prayer for The Dead. 'In your hands, Oh Lord, we humbly entrust our brothers and sisters. In this life you embraced them with your tender love.'"

Kristy felt herself become fidgety. She had to get out of here. Not just the church but out of *here*. Someplace she hadn't been before…

"'Deliver them now from every evil,'" continued Father Smith.

Unexpected things hitting our lives. Kristy continued to think of what she needed now that there was nothing left. Here, flights of fancy became balls of stress. She realized in that moment that there really was nothing she had in her life that she used to decrease stress. She needed a break, a walk, a hideaway.

"'…and bid them eternal rest…welcome them into paradise…with your Son and the Holy Spirit…'" Father Smith continued, but Kristy tuned in and out.

–Old Faces in New Places–

"It was a lovely ceremony. I thought."

Kristy's vision funneled in and out in a blur.

It was Sandra Holbrook, their neighbor from, oh, ten twelve years ago. When Beck was just a tiny thing.

"Huh?" Mumbled Kristy, not meaning to seem rude but probably coming across as such.

"I said, I thought it was a lovely ceremony. And, Kristy, I am so terribly sorry."

With a half-hearted, but as enthusiastic as she could muster, smile she patted Sandra on the shoulder and walked up the aisle towards the caskets.

There were about twenty people remaining in the church, all in all. Kristy tried to make eye contact with none of them.

Sandra just looked on as Kristy vacantly reached the caskets.

How morbid, Kristy would think repeatedly and sporadically throughout her life, to parade their bodies in front of everyone. Just the general concept of an open casket...morbid. Why not just bury them and then hold the ceremony? Some men from the mortuary approached both her and the caskets. With a respectful glance the two of them moved their eyes to match her gaze then back down to the carpet surrounding the priest's podium. They gave her time to stare at what was once her family. Now more resembling the stuffed birds from *Psycho* than the life she had helped build. The life he had deconstructed.

16

She glanced up at the mortuary workers, nodded, and made her way back down the aisle, brushing past all of the other attendees. Everyone in the building stared at her. Kristy could feel it like acid eating through skin. All looked on in worry, save for two.

–Filters–

How did she lose time again? This is what paraded
through Kristy's mind on repeat. She was in her car, now.
She remembered the aisle, but, just that brief bit of space
from the church to her car…a blur.

She held her head and dragged her fingers down her
face, pulling down her lower eyelids in the process. There
was red not just below her eyes, but within them. She was
exhausted. Yeah, that was all.

Another rapping on the window.

Mom in law again. Oh, the weather outside…

No, someone else. The blurry vision again. Sandra Holbrook, with her stretched-out face and beehive haircut. To Kristy she always seemed like a woman of a different time, despite being only a few years older. At a time, she had been a local beauty pageant winner. Some said she still could be. Age benefits some better than others but, Kristy, well, Kristy didn't see it.

She looked to her for a moment, then looked all around the exterior of the church. No one else, not even Casey or Craig. How odd. She figured there would be other stragglers, though, with that being said, who knew how long she had been sitting in the car.

"You know," Sandra said before a breath after Kristy rolled the window down, "there are filters."

Filters? What? Kristy thought.

19

"Filters? What?" Kristy asked.

"Everything we do, we see; we can't adjust what happens, but we can adjust our filters."

Kristy rubbed her face again, though this time her exhaustion was with a woman she had only seen rarely for the past decade or so.

"Yeah, and how do you suggest I do that for this particular situation, Mrs. Holbrook?"

"Ms., now, and we can adjust our filters for anything. Well, you know where I've been…not the same as you, but, similar. I mean, I still have my Becky."

She had totally forgotten. Two years and some change back, Sandra's husband had died quickly and unceremoniously in a car accident too. Deckland had gone to the funeral because the two of them were drinking buddies. Kristy hadn't made the funeral, but Deckland had taken Beck, who was more or less a friend to the girl. At least, that's what she thought she remembered.

"I'm only here," said Sandra, "because our kids were so close. I know how you feel about me and, take my word, the feeling's mutual."

Kristy raised an eyebrow. How direct Sandra was. This was not a quality she remembered being a primary component of Sandra's personality. What she wanted to say was *Ms. Holbrook, I don't feel one way or another about you.*

Instead, she stammered.

"Well...I..."

"No, no, no, sweetie, it's fine. Look, I was hoping to change that. Now we have, similar blood, circumstances, I mean."

21

"Ah, uh, maybe. Look, though, I'm not in a place for new friends." She knew she should say more but instead she put her car in reverse and moved out of the church's parking lot.

That was, until a horn honked. Lights were flashing and Kristy swerved before bashing front bumper to front bumper with an eighteen-wheeler.

Time lost. Again.

In an instant she was on the curb, watching honking cars with angry drivers go by as she screamed to the windshield and then wiped the tears from her face. *Coffee, please sweet shit I need some coffee.*

And then, in a flash, she was staring at her Keurig, brewing coffee. Once she got her internal navigator working again on the side of the road, got a grip on her surroundings, she realized that she was quite close to home. The rest of the drive went smoothly.

But what had been a dream? The driving and near-accident? Sandra? Both? Neither?

Whatever surety she had of reality was now laughable.

That's when *more* rapping startled her. Though, this time, it came not from her car's window, but on her home's front door.

As she lumbered out of the kitchen, then through the living room, she bumped into the ottoman. She had to wake up, get it together. She moved slowly, more cautiously, placing her hand on the wall for balance, and grabbed the door knob. She twisted, then pulled, twisted, then pulled, never thinking to unlock it first.

When she opened it, Casey and Craig were looking at the doorknob, having clearly been perplexed by her seeming inability to fulfill the basic function of unlocking the door prior to opening it. Where was her mind, they must be thinking.

Craig offered a smile while Casey offered a scowl.

Without asking, Casey pushed into the house, stopping to pick up a picture of her son off the foyer table.

She stared at it as Craig put his hand on Kristy's shoulder, quickly removing it as Casey looked back.

"I'm getting a drink," Casey said dully as if her entire existence were currently on autotune. "Who wants a drink?" She pointed to Kristy, "you?" She pointed to her husband, "dearest? No? No, I thought not."

Craig looked over with what appeared to Kristy to be mounting worry with a splash of anger.

As Casey left the foyer, moved through the living room, and made her way into the kitchen, Craig smiled to his daughter-in-law once again. A sheepish, embarrassed smile. "You'll have to forgive her. Well, you know. You of all people. I think we all have backbones, partly made up of the people we care about…" he droned off and looked onto the kitchen. Neither Kristy nor Craig could see Casey but heard her rummaging through the freezer, then moving her way to the blender. As it whirred, he turned back to Kristy.

"I could never be that backbone for her."

"I couldn't for your son. So, we're on level terrain."

"No. Hon', no we're not. You were his backbone, you and Beck. But, some people, they just can't take all of this. Your husband was like that and there really wasn't anything you could do. He was like his mother."

He looked back to the kitchen with longing yet an air of resentment.

"Being a mother was her backbone, not being a wife, having a husband. But, in truth, she failed. She taught him everything he knew about self-destruction. I think part of her knows that. Now her backbone is broken, and…her

26

grandson…" he trailed off again upon seeing Kristy's face grow rigid.

He threw his arms around her gently, his thumbs rubbing her shoulder blades. "No matter what, you'll always be my daughter. I never had a daughter, until you. Stop blaming yourself, stop hating yourself. But, remember them. I'm afraid you're not doing that now. Today, you just, seemed gone." He paused to take note of Kristy's look of understanding. She also looked as if she were stifling a thought or two. "Take a breather, that's what we're doing. Rent an Air B-n-B. We did it—you knew this—not too long back. Went to Maine? You knew about this, right?"

"Yeah, sounded lovely."

"It was. My point is, get out of town. Get out of your own life for a bit. Try to get out of your own head, even. Please try."

"Did it work for you two?"

"What, the vacation?"

"Getting out of your heads."

"Sort of, we've gotten along better, at least until this."

"Doubt it'll work for me and her."

"Honey we live in a world where people question Ruth Bader Ginsburg's ethics mere minutes after she's died. In this world, nothing is impossible. Except *that*, I'm afraid."

Father-in-law and daughter-in-law laughed in unison, but stifled it as Casey re-entered the room.

"What's funny." She phrased it hardly even as a question. Her disinterest shone like the aurora borealis. "What're y'all talking about?"

"Oh, hon', just our vacation. The Air BnB. Don't you think that's a good idea for her?"

"Sure." Casey sipped her margherita and mumbled, "a vacation from your vacation."

"Honey. Enough. We talked about this."

"What'd I say? I didn't even say anything."

"Casey," Kristy said, "is there a *reason* you're here? Want some pictures of Deck and Beck?"

"Well, I'm sure you don't need the ones of Decky, now, do you?"

"Hon!" Screamed Craig, startling his wife enough to cause her to spill some of her sugary drink on the carpet.

Craig started rubbing his head. Casey looked genuinely concerned, put her margherita down on the foyer table, and approached Craig. He only pushed her away.

"Casey, this isn't easy for anyone." He said with his hands still covering his eyes. "Can't you see I'm dealing with this too? I'm tired too? Well *she's* tired, too."

Casey looked like ice.

"She's dealing with the same thing you are. She's lost a son" he raised an apologetic hand in Kristy's direction and razor focused his eyes on his wife. "She's no different than you now. I know you. I know that when a line has been crossed you just gotta find out who crossed it but this time the only one who crossed a line was *our* son. There's nothing we can do about that now. You don't even need to

support her. But what you can do is climb off of her fucking

back, Casey! If you're not building bridges, which you

aren't, you're putting up walls and walls don't accomplish a

goddamned thing."

For a few moments, Casey stood there thunderstruck

by her normally silent husband. Then, without warning, she

slapped him and burst through the front door. It slammed

behind her. Craig looked up to Kristy with tears in his eyes.

Kristy knew the tears weren't from the smack, but from a

much deeper wound.

"If not now, when, right?" He asked rhetorically.

Kristy just stood there, comparably thunderstruck.

Craig reached in his pocket and pulled out a wad of

hundreds. "She doesn't know about this, but, like I

31

said…leave yourself for a bit. Survive, like I'm not sure I can. I love you, m'dear. Be well."

Wadded up with the cash was a note: *The Hamilton House. Air BnB. Worth It. It's close to us and if you need anything call me.*

With that he turned and opened the front door and took steady steps out. Kristy held open the door and watched him descend the concrete steps and make his way to the car, which Casey was leaning on. Kristy heard no sobbing, she just saw her leaning over the roof, almost as if she passed out that way.

Kristy closed the door and went back into the kitchen. She sipped from her cup and grimaced.

She'd have to make a new cup of coffee.

–An Easy Trip–

At 8 A.M., the light was just beginning to show over the mountains. Kristy had told herself, in a sort of haphazard and futile personal strength technique, that she wouldn't light up the day's first cigarette until her headlights were no longer necessary.

The dawn wasn't quite there, but it was close enough. While keeping her eyes on the road, her hand fumbled over the latch of the glove box until she managed to grab hold and pull it open. Her hand moved over her wallet and registration. She pulled them up, tossed them over, and grabbed her pack of cigarettes intentionally placed at the very bottom of the glovebox.

With shaking hands, she tossed them to the passenger's seat, put her hand back in the glovebox until she found the lighter, used her right pinky and ring finger to close the glovebox and tossed the lighter next to the pack on the passenger's seat.

As she passed a stony, mountainous hill to her right, movement caught her attention to the wooded left. A deer stood solitary and stagnant, moving its gaze along with the movement of her vehicle. Their eyes matched, and a positive thought rolled through Kristy's mind. It wouldn't be unthinkable for the deer to have been in the road, or for her gaze to have been affixed on the glovebox, or both.

Then, a negative thought. *Would it matter?*

She shook it off and replaced it with another: herself, Deckland and Beck watching *Pulp Fiction* together. Beck had already seen it sans her permission anyway, so they might as well share it since her opinion on what her son was allowed to watch was apparently not up to her.

Afterwards, Beck had turned around, flashed what they all called "the Bambi eyes" and asked if they could watch another movie. Sitting in her car, Kristy laughed as she remembered her response: "Pretty please, with sugar on top, do your freakin' homework", a reference to a line in the film delivered by Harvey Keitel.

Both Deckland and Beck had laughed. Beck had then risen, kissed his mother and said "Well done" with another chuckle.

In the car, Kristy began to chuckle as well, then burst out laughing to the point tears began rolling down her cheeks. Then, they were mixed with other tears, from different receptors of her brain. She pulled her car over into the thin bit of pavement between the empty road and the guard rail. After she slowly exited the vehicle, she grabbed the guard rail and, with cloudy eyes, peered over to see a nearly endless hill bottoming out to the sight of mixed, leafy, tree tops. She fell to her knees, with her right hand on the top of three steel rails, her left on top of the center steel rail, and wept.

—

All she could hear was the whining of a slowing vehicle with failing brakes. Then, nothing.

36

"Ma'am," rang out a voice, echoing across the open vista despite having been spoken at low volume.

She adjusted her gaze to the right to see a young, African American man in a light blue shirt.

"Miss, you okay?"

Kristy rolled her hand across her eyes and gave a brief, polite smile. "Fine, thanks."

"Okay, good. Well, this isn't safe. Vehicles aren't permitted here, save for a breakdown. Is your car broken down?"

"No, I just...needed a moment."

He leaned against the guard rail, peering down briefly then raising his vision up, as if the sight of the shattering woman was a bit much for him.

"Okay, well, again, sorry to disturb."

"It's fine, not much of your business, but fine."

For a beat, taken aback, he said nothing.

"Ah, but it is. Officer Chet Williams, highway patrol." He looked down to his shirt, then back up with a smile, "off duty, currently."

"Oh, I see. Well, get to work, then." Her tone was grave, irritated. Some moments shouldn't be interrupted.

"Mmhmm," he mumbled as he walked back to what must have been his off-duty vehicle. Without looking back, he said, "have a *safe* day ma'am."

With another whine from his car as it got into gear, he drove past her. "I'm sorry," she said too late as he moved down the road. She gave a wave, hoping he would see it. She had no idea if he in fact did.

–Home Away from Home–

She had to admit, it was gorgeous. It was all just as

the pictures on the site had made it out to be. After

travelling about a mile and a half on an uphill driveway she

had reached the Air BnB. The cabin where she would be

temporarily residing sat to the left of the main house, where

the hostess would be, of course, residing, with about thirty

feet in between.

Both structures contained a screened in porch

essentially facing one another but slightly cattycornered.

The structures were not level with one another as between

them there was one final little hill. This made it so the

house's porch sat about a foot, perhaps just less, above the porch of the cabin.

The hostess had promised that they would barely see each other, and Kristy was beginning to take this quite literally as there was no one in sight save for a few clucking chickens at the bottom of the hill below the cabin, next to the end of the driveway and her now-parked car.

She walked past the front door of the cabin, rounded the structure and moved past the porch, then rounded the cabin again to see the rear. Nearly the entirety of the back wall of the cabin was covered by a thick, leafy trellis. A pathway served as a border between the cabin and the house. Looking at the trellis to the left, then to the other on her right, she looked up to see a roofing structure connecting the two. It was an arbor. In terms of the side next to the cabin, the trellis extended farther than the roof of the arbor, leading up to and stopping at the roof of the cabin. It could be used as a ladder, though this would be strongly discouraged by the manufacturer.

"Hello?" A thick, nearly baritone woman's voice rang down from above.

Kristy jumped and looked up the trellis touching the cabin.

Peering down was a woman with short red hair and what her father would have described as a shit eating grin.

Reserve the judgment, Kristy, reserve it. She plastered a smile across her face and waited as the woman descended the trellis. With each step it thumped against the cabin. Kristy placed her fingers through one of the holes in the wood trellis and stabilized it.

"Oh, Mylanta!" The woman chuckled. Then, with a hop, she reached the pebble walkway and immediately extended her hand.

"Reba Fahey, you must be Kristy Northam".

Kristy extended her right hand in accepting reply. "Northram. Don't worry, common mistake."

"Well Miss Northram—"

"Please, Kristy is fine."

"Kristy," Reba kept her smile wide, "please, call me Reba. Can I show you around?"

"Absolutely. Beautiful property, Reba, simply stunning."

"It does me well," Reba nearly giggled. "Okay, well as Steven Tyler once screamed, 'walk this way'." The pebbles of the walkway were strewn aside their footfalls in near unison as they made their way down. "I'm hardly ever here, and now that I am you still won't see me much save for when I'm feeding those little clumps of feathers down there."

"I saw them. So cute. You're hardly ever here? My God, how do you leave?" Kristy nodded her head up past the surrounding forest to the north side where a wide-open view of a mountain sat. She found it stunning, as did most, if not all, who saw it.

"I guess I've slowed down on travelling in recent years, but yes, I'm here, oh, five months of the year."

"And the other seven?"

"Travelling, always. While that still sounds like a lot, trust me, it's a cut back."

"I read the bio on your Air BnB page—part of the reason why I chose this place, actually—about your work background. You're a writer?"

"Travel writer. I didn't see a bio on your end but you mentioned you planned on doing some writing as well?"

"Merely as a means of catharsis. I can't claim to be a professional."

"Trade secret. Even the professionals write as a means of catharsis. It's just sometimes they get to cash a check."

"How did you get started in the travel writing circle?"

"My husband."

They came to the end of the descending pebble walkway, reaching the end of the driveway—if one were driving up to the cabin—and the chickens. Reba reached to a wooden platform and removed a plastic jug filled with chicken feed. Sitting atop the feed was a scooper which she used to dispense food to the six chickens. They rushed forward, two of them came from out of the little red painted barn, clucking excitedly.

Throughout it all, Kristy merely thought of the words *my husband*.

"I hesitate to ask," said Reba, breaking through the permeating silence, "but what requires catharsis?"

For a very palpable few moments, Kristy remained silent. It seemed a bit soon for her to ask such a question, but she didn't want Reba to feel as if her question was out of line.

"Back home, back in Crockett…" Kristy trailed off as she noticed a look of recognition on Reba's face.

"I'm familiar with Crockett, beautiful little town."

"It is. Very little."

Reba smiled and Kristy continued, "the town council is debating changing a street name from an historic—albeit racist—figure to my son's name."

Reba's face lost the smile, and drooped, recognizing that such a debate, not to mention gesture, would only arise from a death. She extended her arm, nervously, to Kristy's shoulder and said, "oh my."

"Yeah. My thoughts exactly. Anyway, if you can believe it, many want the racist historical figure's name to remain."

Reba chortled in an agreeing, condescending, "of course they do" kind of way.

"Right? But truth be told, I don't care either way. I'm fine with the name of the street being changed, it's not as if I want to celebrate racism, but…I don't want to drive down the street and…"

"Have the reminder?"

"Exactly."

"I can't blame you in the least, sweetie. I'm so sorry. We can change the subject, if you like?"

"It's fine, but perhaps that'd be for the best."

"Fine, fine. What do you do to bring in the bacon, as my husband would have said?"

"School counselor, I specialize in group dynamics."

"Certainly a fine environment for group dynamics. Schools, I mean. What grade set?"

"Middle."

"Oh man. Talk about group emotional development. Perpetually chaotic group emotional development."

Kristy chortled, "some of the staff aren't fully developed themselves."

Reba burst out laughing, "preaching to the converted. I used to have a bullshit government job and frequently felt like the sanest person in the building."

Both paused, listening to the clucking chickens. Kristy wrapped her arms around her torso. "I doubt I'll go back. I'm already thinking that now; I guarantee you after three days being here, away from it, I'll be thinking it more."

"There's nothing wrong with a change."

"Oh, well, I guess you'd know." Kristy's tone came across almost flat, or at least that's how she perceived it judging by Reba's raised brow.

"How do you mean?"

"Huh? Just going from government work to travel writing."

"Oh! Ah, yes. Quite a one-eighty. From being behind a desk from the seventeen-hundreds to travelling to seventeen hundred different places."

Kristy smiled. Still, her grip on her torso tightened.

49

"I'm really here to break repetition. I'll tell ya, if I tell one more student 'With every group comes a diversity of purpose. There's a door. Sometimes that door opens and in comes somebody who can fulfill the purpose better than an existing member. That'll always ruffle feathers.' And have them give me that wide, hazy-eyed, mouth-agape look…my office windows will require bars."

"Well, I can't blame them, that's a mouthful!" Reba said through a laugh.

As they both laughed, Kristy thought of how odd it was that she felt so comfortable discussing such personal matters with a stranger. Still, there was something about Reba. Some people just don't feel like strangers.

Reba looked up to the cabin. "So, let's do the full tour. As stated on the webpage, you'll be left alone with your catharsis all you need. I'll be here throughout the weekend and, again, you'll either see me with the chickens or back there." She flicked her thumb over her shoulder to the garage. It was a triple wide with electric sliding doors. "My garage is also my workspace; I'm sure you noticed the bike."

"Huh? No."

They moved towards the garage where one door was all the way open. Inside sat a motorcycle with numerous tools all around it along with a workbench. A socket wrench sat on the cushion seat. As they entered the garage, Kristy looked around and noticed tools hung all over the wall. Sitting behind the center electric door was a Ford Mustang. Yellow, classic, but Kristy knew very little about it outside of its classic status.

"Just a time killer, more than anything," Reba said. "It's a hobby I picked up from my husband, before he passed."

"Oh, I'm so sorry." Kristy paused. "Do you mind if I ask how?"

"Car accident."

Kristy's hairs on the back of her neck leapt up, rigid.

"I understand," Kristy said. "But, that's neat…you doing something with it, I mean."

"Yeah, I suppose." She turned with a smile, "ready to see the cabin?"

Struck a nerve. Shit, thought Kristy.

"Absolutely," she replied before her pause became noticeable.

As they left the garage, Reba tapped a button just before the door, resulting in it lowering, fully sealing the garage. "Usually I use the clicker, but I left it in the house."

They passed the driveway and walked up the steep provisional sidewalk to the cabin, which was really just a series of flat stones intermittently laid down with grass poking up between each. Halfway up, to their right, was a decrepit firepit. It didn't look like it had been used in quite a while.

"If you'd like," said Reba as she paused next to the firepit, "you can make a fire this evening or, well, any other evening you're here. That's fair game. I haven't used it in some time, been waiting for it to get a bit colder out. You live a little further south, right? Probably used to it being a bit warmer so the evenings may feel cooler to you than they do me."

"I imagine I just might. We'll see how it gets in the evening."

"I usually wait until October. Though, I guess we're only a month or so from that anyway. You see that?" Reba pointed to an enclosed, wooden, miniature shed. It stood about five feet high and four feet wide with a chained-shut, green roof. "That's a firewood rack, I nailed that sheet metal slab on top of the wood roof to keep the rain out. In fact, the roof of the cabin has slabs of the same on top, though thicker. Anyway, the wood should be good to go."

"Excellent, that's great."

The steps to the cabin creaked as Reba then Kristy walked up them. Reba pulled the storm door, then, with a slight kick, pushed open the front door. "In the mornings I get eggs from the chickies, so if you like eggs…" She moved towards the refrigerator just beyond the six-foot foyer which contained only a small, round dining table with surrounding stools and a book shelf just behind it, hugging the brief bit of wall before the space opened up. The book shelf contained board games and a few of Reba's travel guide books with a lower portion serving as a thicker cabinet.

Reba opened the refrigerator door and looked in. "Yeah, good, I put in some fresh eggs just yesterday so tomorrow you should have breakfast waiting already. There's bread in the cupboard, coffee pods just next to the bread. I assume you brought some food as well?"

"I did...really I didn't plan on all this. This is wonderful, thank you."

Reba shot a proud smile and Kristy hoped she didn't come across as rushing her off. In truth, she thought, she usually would be. But, she far from minded Reba's company. They turned to their left and scanned the remainder of the cabin. First, Kristy moved towards the bookshelf and picked up one of the books, titled *Toledo: The Must Do's.* She scanned the cover, flipped it to the back to see Reba's image, though with her red hair longer.

Reba picked up a book from a stack of identical books laying face up—as opposed to the traditional binding out—flat on the lower, protruding cabinet portion of the shelf. "This is the one I did on the Blue Ridge Mountains. All of my guests are permitted to take one, should you feel so inclined. It's not gonna blow your skirt up or win me a Pulitzer but it can be helpful."

Kristy chuckled and said, "I promise I will."

Reba put the book down, put her hands in her jeans'

pockets and looked up. There was a spiral staircase that led

to the second level, which comprised only half the length of

the cabin. The far side from the kitchen was an open space

made up two stories, the near side, towards the kitchen,

contained a separate floor above, an upstairs bedroom.

Above both sides was an attic, with its pull down

entranceway just a few feet above the height of the bed, and

a few feet diagonal from the bed's foot.

Kristy lowered her gaze back to Reba, who placed

the keys on the table of the tiny foyer. As she opened the

front door she turned back to Kristy, she flashed her right

thumb to another door to the right of the refrigerator. "Out

there is the porch–"

"I saw, I bet it's terrific for coffee in the mornings."

"My thoughts exactly. The only time you'll for sure see me is when I'm doing the same on my porch."

"Well, if you'd like, I'm making a meatloaf this evening. I plan on eating it on the porch."

After a pause, Reba said, "okay. I'd love to. But save the meatloaf, I'll make sandwiches and a treat to boot."

"Terrific.

"Any preference for the 'wiches?"

"No, no anything's fine."

Reba nodded, left the cabin and Kristy thought about how out of the blue the invitation had been, how unusual for her to initiate. She could spend time mulling it over, but, as she looked at her watch and read the short hand on the 10 and the long hand on the 17, she had the oddest feeling that now would be a good time for a nap. Early as it may be, she felt wiped.

—

Kristy sat in her office chair. When things became too dull, which was frequently, she would swivel round and round. Her office was almost too small to move, just about the size of two cubicles one next to the other. It was enough for her and one client, maybe two with some stuffing in for a conflict resolution session. Those were few and far between. Usually, it was just a one-on-one session, with Kristy futilely instructing middle schoolers about the intricacies of being in a group.

On this day, she was with a kid named Bryce, though, she was never supposed to reveal the names of her clients. She never did, but she always wanted to talk about Bryce. But, with whom?

Most came into her office stifling tears because they were being teased or excluded. Usually, that was the result of behavior from kids like Bryce or, just as frequently, Bryce himself. "It's important to have empathy, Bryce," she nearly moaned, recognizing that this was just a variation of a conversation she had had with him ad nauseum.

Bryce stared back; arms crossed.

"Think small, okay? Then large. You never know how someone's morning was. You've had bad mornings, right?"

"Sure."

"Can't you imagine that someone else might feel the same? Maybe their morning was *awful*. Well, multiple that by 365, then multiply that by, how old are you, fourteen?"

Bryce nodded.

"Then multiply that by fourteen. The point is, some people have bad days most days. Imagine that. Imagine how that would feel to *you*."

"I wouldn't care."

Yeah, I bet you wouldn't. If the mind's eye could roll...

"Bryce, it's okay to fe—"

"Can I go now?"

She had lost him. The point had gotten away from her, especially when she knew why this kid had such…bad mornings, such tendency to lash out. We are our parents' children. But maybe that was too simplistic an explanation. If she dug deeper maybe it'd be too complex. Maybe some kids are just incapable of coping.

Kristy woke up in a sweat. These were the thoughts of burnout, and these were the thoughts she had had. Defeatist thoughts parading as realism. Her watch read 2:41.

She whipped out her journal. Her hand grasped the pen and shook over the paper with no words written. For a few minutes, there still were no words written. Her mind echoed within itself until a waking dream arose. A recurring dream, but never one she had at night.

Her husband, sober, walking up a grassy hill to Beck's high school graduation. Beck turning, nodding to his father like "thanks for coming, Dad" and just walking the stage. Her watch now read 3:27.

Did I lose time, again?!

Then, with some semblance of recognition, she remembered just after the funeral, a few days prior, when she had lost time. Now, she had the time again, unearthed from the recesses of her trap door mind. She stood in front of Deckland's grave, making eye contact only with it, not the grave next to it—her eyes averted the sight of the next grave over via pure instinct, a pure aversion to pain.

You could have done it. You could have cut the shit. At least slowed down on it. And you would've been able to see him cross that stage, ready for the world. Instead, now, I won't even be able to see him do it. Fuck you, Deck. Fuck you and fuck whomever you were screwing. You think I didn't know the smell. Sweat and latex. It's unmistakable, you rat mothe—

Kristy awoke. Groggy and disoriented she came to realize that the feeling of waking, holding her notebook, it had been a part of the dream. She looked to the end table next to the bed. The notebook was still there. She had no memory of placing it there nor any memory of even ascending the staircase, climbing into bed.

As she lay there, she flicked the toes on her feet left, then right, and so on. A physical mannerism she employed to combat anxiety. With even the simplest thing, such as a twitch, she felt content. This place really wasn't so bad.

She checked her watch.

5:36, I slept all day.

Suddenly there were two bangs on the door. Kristy got up from the bed and made her way to the top of the spiral staircase when two more wraps on the door echoed throughout the cabin. Then, from behind her a SMASH. With a jump, she stumbled forward until her stomach bumped into the staircase's guardrail. She turned, shaking head to toe, to see the attic's entryway door wide open, the metal ladder extended down to the floor, and a sealing chain dangling from the ceiling to the right.

"Jesus," she eked out.

There was the sound of keys jingling in the front door, then the bottom of the door sliding on the wood, as if it was pulling up tiny oak shavings. "Kristy?!"

"Ah, uh, it was the attic, uh, door."

"Oh, my goodness I am so sorry. Are you hurt?"

Kristy made her way to the bottom of the staircase and met Reba face to face.

Kristy paused before rubbing her head and saying, "No, I'm okay."

"It must have been the wind over the past few days that loosened it, the knocking that let it give way. I'm just glad you aren't hurt."

Kristy gave a little shake and a smile. "Me too, close call." She laughed.

Reba was holding a serving platter with sandwiches and pecan brownies, which she placed on the small, round foyer table. "Gimme a second."

Kristy sat at the table as Reba went upstairs and, judging by the metallic sliding sound and the thump, closed the attic doorway. She looked over to the sandwiches and brownies. Homemade, it was a nice touch. Then, there were a series of footsteps as Reba descended the staircase, nearly bouncing. "It's sealed tight now. Shouldn't happen again. That's never happened before, biggest problem I've ever had with it is the ladder comes down, just, *way* too fast. I always have to brace myself, hold my hand out to catch it."

Kristy pulled out a brownie from under the saranwrap and took a bite. "Delicious, hope you don't mind."

Reba laughed, "oh well, that's where it's going anyway. Shall we go out on the porch?"

"Absolutely," Kristy said.

67

–Warmth & Comfort–

Kristy flipped her phone, seeing two bars' signal.

"You get reception out here okay?" Reba asked.

"It seems to flicker in and out. Can't say I need it anyway."

"That's the spirit. It took me a while to get used to that, until I realized there's nothing on the phone I want that I don't have here."

She waved her hand in an arc, indicating the surrounding forestation vista.

"Yeah, I need to get my mind away from it."

Reba nodded and took a bite of her sandwich. After she swallowed, she said, "The only thing I like about modern technology is the chat option for customer service. I prefer to read my clearly scripted answers instead of hear them from a disinterested twenty-three-year-old after waiting five hours."

Kristy laughed, "Totally agree. Plus, I like how it says 'prefer to chat'? I imagine that in a British voice. Love it!"

From the rear of the cabin, just out of view of them both, fingers went through two of the gaps in the leafy trellis. Below the arbor, a figure. Wind blew brown and red leaves all over as the first rumble of thunder for the evening roared far away, beyond the mountain to the north.

"Are you liking it here, so far?"

Kristy didn't quite become startled by the thunder, but took a moment to answer. "Very much so, I took a nap in the middle of the day. I can't tell you the last time I did that."

"Right? This area is so conducive to that. I always feel like a lazy piece of—" Reba cut herself off. "But, it's worth it."

Both women laughed.

"I've gotten some thinking done, too," Kristy said with a pause, "I think."

"I'm glad. You get some catharsis out of it?"

"I think so. I mean, I know there's no answer that…I know there's just what's next. I think a few days here will help; I really do."

"Y'know, I was checking the site…I don't have anyone staying here for a few days."

Kristy raised a brow. *Money gouging, that seems unlike her.*

As if through second sight, Reba laughed and held up a hand with a brownie placed between her thumb and index finger. "No, no, don't worry. I've never done this but I genuinely just like having you around," Reba said with an air of self-aware awkwardness that actually mirrored the approximate feelings of Kristy.

"Honestly, I feel the same way. This is my first Air BnB, I assume the same can't be said for you?"

"Oh, no, I've had about forty guests thus far."

"Well, I'm touched, and as long as no one else signs up for after my last day–and I can pay you, of course—"

Reba waved this off, eliciting a warm smile from Kristy. Much to her surprise, she felt at home, more so even than her own home had made her feel from time to time.

"Thank you, Reba."

"For what it's worth, I put two and two together, I'm sorry about your son."

With a shy, quick glance, Kristy shot a smile. "And your husband, too."

"Thank you," said Reba with an equally shy and quick glance. "Are *you* married? I'm sorry, I don't mean to push."

"No, and don't worry. But, no, not married."

"I see."

No, you don't. Nor should you.

"It's fine, really." Kristy said after the quick mull in her mind.

She continued, "If more people in this world gave a shit, the machinery would run with less rust. My husband was never one to do that."

Reba only nodded a few times, which Kristy respected. This woman knew how best to not push.

Finally, Reba said, "Y'know, my daddy once told me 'You can choose how to live, but with all that goes wrong this world don't let you choose how to survive.' So far, I think you're doing okay."

The pause between the two was perceptible before Kristy almost squeaked out, "Your daddy sounds like he was a wise man."

"He was. Irony being he didn't always give a shit. But he had an excuse. Vietnam took *several* tolls on him."

"And many others. Same for now, I guess."

"Oh, God, I'll tell ya, I can take but so much of the current political landscape. It's made me love the isolation up here even more. Can you imagine living in D.C. now? Lordy."

"I'd rather be a corpse."

With a chuckle, Reba said, "Y'ain't alone. Life is unexpected. Sometimes that's what keeps it interesting, livable, sometimes the total opposite."

To further cement the feeling that the two of them were in sync, both shivered as a breeze rolled through the screened in porch, and another echoing roar of thunder ripped above them. "I think I'll call it a night, Kristy. You have everything you need for the evening?"

All of a sudden, with an echo of impending loneliness ripping through her like a warning bell, Kristy wanted a cigarette. She came here for isolation, yet the knowledge that soon it would be just her was…frightening. That little ball of anxiety deep within her started to expand, metastasize.

While Kristy felt tired as well, having stuffed herself with some particularly good sandwiches, the thought of being alone gave her that irreplaceably repulsive shudder that comes with the sinking knowledge that you just drank a fly with your coffee. "Oh, I've got more than enough. I don't think I'll be making a fire tonight. May turn in, like you said."

"Very good," Reba said as she got up from the creaking rocking chair. "Tell you what, we can do S'more's tomorrow night."

"Sounds wonderful. Good night, Reba."

With a final smile, Reba exited the porch, and the screen door slapped the entranceway wood once, then softer, then softer but still with a clang.

—

As Kristy entered, she heard the rumbling of her vibrating phone on the foyer table.

"Christ, what now?"

The screen read: 1 NEW MESSAGE.

She typed in her code and listened. It was Casey.

Oh, the weather outside is frightful—

Another boom of thunder. This one made her jump. While feeling silly, she decided to focus on the words of her mother-in-law.

The message began with a huff. "Kristy. I've spoken with Craig and perhaps, *perhaps*, I was rough on you yesterday. For that I apologize. Please know that I don't *blame* you for anything, and hope we can build a…" Dead air, as if she were reading through a cue card before returning, "relationship that can keep the memory of Deckland and Beck alive. Have a good evening." Click.

Kristy figured one of two things were true: Craig threatened to leave her ass if she didn't apologize, or, she wanted something.

Either way, man did Kristy want a cigarette.

She went outside, lit up, took a few drags, and felt...sick?

Unusual.

But the light buzz was worth it, especially in tandem with the view of the stars. Before long, she figured it was time for bed.

–Whoever Said Sleep is For the Dead was an Idiot–

She dreamed. Her mind was a Dairy Queen Blizzard, yet…thicker and more congested.

She saw her husband. Standing still, hands in pockets.

"You live in fear," Deckland said.

"Why, Deck? Wasn't I enough? Why wasn't I enough? What are you going to tell me now? Fear…that's no way to live? Are you the ghost of Christmas past?"

"Honey, fear…out here that's the only way to live." Deckland said as Kristy woke to the shaking, but not shattering, of the window cattycorner to the bedframe.

79

Something. Someone was downstairs. She could

hear footsteps.

Heavy, yet measured.

She rose from the bed, and with cautious steps

moved her way down the staircase, gripping the steel

guiding bars tighter than she'd grabbed Beck as a baby. All

she knew, in this very moment, was fear. For whatever

reason, she despised herself for it. She shouldn't feel

fear…the worst part of her life was over.

All that remained was whatever was next.

She reached the ground level and made her way to

the bathroom. Her eyes were bloodshot. She knew…she

knew this was abnormal. She never had bloodshot eyes.

Wake up at this time, go to sleep at this time. Then the next

day would be the same.

She could have *sworn* she heard someone else in this cabin.

But, as she looked around, not a soul. Not even her dead husband who, oddly enough, was the first person she expected this evening.

Still, she stood in the cabin's narrow bathroom and flicked on the light. There were a few soft popping sounds as the light flickered and, after the fourth flicker, turned on in full.

She moved towards the sink and turned it on. Just as with the light bulb, the faucet took a few seconds to produce a steady stream. Kristy wiped the cool flowing water from the faucet over her brows, let it flow over her eyes, then her cheeks. She looked like she had lived and died before. The mirror betrayed whatever optimism she had.

Another nasty thought.

Having others provides more opportunity to put life in jeopardy. You have no one, you live longer.

She spoke into the mirror, "the trade-off being that longer life isn't worth living."

With one more splash she turned, and made her way the few steps towards the wide-open door of the bathroom. The door had a six-foot mirror, directly opposite the elongated dual mirror for an ostensible couple to brush their teeth. A his and hers...she thought that's what they were called, in the colloquial sense.

Kristy could see her reflection on both sides, the door mirror and the his and hers. Then again, then again, then again as reflection played off of reflection. Then, two sets of arms burst from both panels of glass in unison. They grabbed her equally strong on both sides and shook her. Slapped her.

A scream cut through the delusion. In that moment, she was able to differentiate between the real and fictitious ramblings of her mind. It sounded like…Reba?

And then she shook herself from her groggy state to the sight of a young man. Eighteen, maybe twenty. Short, slick, brown hair. In one hand, he had a two by four chunk of wood. He swung it.

—

"You really don't remember me, do ya, Miss Northram? Let me give you a hint." Ken's grin grew devilishly. "With every group comes a diversity of purpose. There's also a door. Sometime, the door opens and *innnn* comes somebody who can...what was it, Becky?"

He looked over to a girl, almost certainly his age, with short, black hair and glasses. She smirked. Becky then tilted her head, "fulfill the purpose better than an 'existing member'" she said using air quotes.

Ken's grin faded, "that'll always ruffle feathers."

Becky and Ken stared at Kristy.

Ken, shaking, continued, "my feathers were ruffled when my friends bailed on me." He got up, swooping his right leg backwards so he was no longer facing the back of the chair as he rose. "Solid advice, Ms. Northram. Becky?"

Becky picked up the chair and swung it to Kristy's face.

With a crackle, two of the wood cross rails broke from the frame of the chair's back as Kristy, still tied, fell to the floor.

Becky bent down and said, "You know, I was supposed to be in the car with Beck that night."

Ken's brow narrowed and stared at Becky.

"I was supposed to be killed by your piece of shit husband, too. Though, that's not the worst thing he would've done to me, the pig." Then, with a sarcastic tone, "not that you knew about *that*." Becky reached back to the entryway table and grabbed Kristy's cigarettes, removing two from the pack. One she inserted into her own mouth before throwing the pack at Ken.

She bent over and held the other cigarette in front of Kristy's nose. "Mmmm, I bet this would be nice right now. I can see you getting ready to sleep, so, maybe later when the special guest arrives. Wait..." She exaggeratedly cupped a hand over her right ear. "I can hear her now."

A scream ripped through the air. It became shrill just before it underwent the lightning-quick process of being cut off. Kristy knew it had been Reba. A wave of guilt enveloped her as she began dipping her toes in unconsciousness.

Becky flashed Kristy a sickening glance.

The last thing Kristy *saw* before fading out was a smug look on Ken's face. "We're good Samaritans. She told us—we do this—it's more like a mercy to you." The last thing Kristy *felt* before fading out was Ken rubbing the flat end of a blade down her cheek. "But, man, if that doesn't

just take some of the fun out of it."

   Is that what you see as the reality of the situation. That's

pretty frightening, man…but I'll show you real fear.

–Mom–

"Hi, hon'," Kristy heard as her eyes fluttered open.

Oh, the weather outsi-…no. No, it's not Casey. But, that

voice.

Kristy tried to focus, but her vision was still hazy.

Sandra Holbrook placed her hands between Kristy's

legs and pushed down. This pulled the chair back up on its

legs. Kristy coughed with the reverberation of the hobbling

chair bouncing ever so slightly from the ground. She felt a

tooth—at least one tooth—loose in her mouth. Blood

trickled from her lower lip down to her chin.

She spit some of it in Sandra's face, who stumbled back into the foyer table. As she wiped it from her glasses onto her shirt, Kristy asked, "so, what, is this about your kid? Because she *could* have been in the accident between my son and my husband? She wasn't. She wasn't in that accident so what the *fuck* do you want?" Kristy ended with a bark.

"Accident?" A grin grew on Sandra's face. "No, dear, there was no accident."

Becky stood behind her mother, leaning against the bookcase. She looked up with focused doe eyes and a grin like a coyote as she gave Sandra her full attention. Ken stood in the doorway with wide eyes and an open mouth.

"It's five o' clock somewhere. Do. You. Know. Where. Your. Kids. Are?" Said Becky slowly through a growing smirk.

Still hazy-eyed, Kristy's vision moved from Sandra behind her, to Becky. "What," she snapped at the teen.

"You were busy working, remember? Eyes glued to your computer? You didn't even notice me, Beck, and Ken here sneak in with two cases of Bud. You also didn't notice him sneak out to get us more. Though, I must admit, neither Ken nor I drank too much that night. Beck, however, ooh Mrs.– I mean, Ms., now–Northram...Beck could put them away."

"Just like his father," said Sandra.

There was a tense pause. Without turning to face her daughter, but with her head turned at a ninety-degree angle

90

so she was in her peripheral vision, Sandra asked, "was that the only way he was like his father, dear?"

"No. He was forceful, too. Didn't like to hear the word 'no'."

Sandra nodded her head. "You knew your husband *raped* me and…nothing. You didn't even *try* to get him into an AA meeting much less a jail cell!"

"It wasn't rape, Sandra. You and I both know that. You got the same way he did at parties. I just couldn't stomach watching him seal the deal with you. It was ten years ago and you were touching him at that hor d'oeuvres table just as much as he was you."

"Still, you defend him! Your husband *cheated on you* and not even a divorce, which you very much should have done. Your husband, my husband, they were something

91

else. But you, Kristy, you are weak. So, two years ago, I took your beloved husband in like he was my own…" Sandra paused then condescendingly and overtly pantomimed hugging, "nurtured him, subtly browbeat him until he kept upping his booze records."

Sandra just stood with her rear against the foyer table, smiling, before she continued, "he really did set a new record that night. I sent him on his way home after Becky confirmed that, yes, in fact, your idiot of a son had gone out to get more beer when, duh, they already had some more. Both so eager to please."

This was the first moment Sandra noticed Kristy flexing her fists. "Someone's mad," said Becky. She noticed too.

Only Kristy knew that this wasn't about anger. Not until now at least. Houdini would flex every muscle in his body to loosen his bindings just enough to be able to slip them off and complete his trick.

Suddenly, she broke loose from her binding, spun to pick up the chair and pushed its legs in front of her as Sandra thrusted a knife sitting on the foyer table towards her. It moved between two of the back rails of the chair, which Kristy yanked to the right, sending the knife tumbling to the floor. The middle two of the four back rails broke in half.

With just as quick a motion, Kristy bashed the chair into Sandra's face, sending her tumbling back to Becky. As Ken lunged towards her, Kristy dove, picked up the knife, and held it to his face. Ken froze and held up his hands as if giving up. She kept her focus on him and, with her other hand, picked up one of the loose rails. She distracted him by briskly thrusting the knife towards his face, sending him backing up just before she stabbed the back rail into his shin. She let go and began to back up, first at a snail's pace, then ever so slightly faster until she felt her ankle bump into the first step of the spiral staircase.

Ken howled and reached down to the back rail, which was a little of halfway through his shin.

With a jerk she spun and burst up the narrow, awkward staircase. On the second to last stair, her toes became caught and she tripped. In the nick of time, she turned the blade of the knife to the right, to avoid stabbing her face in the fall. Without looking back, she heard Ken's clunking footfalls and pushed herself up, leaping for the attic entryway's drawstring.

With her palm held out to stop the unwieldy latter from bashing her face, she leapt up the eight metallic stairs two at a time until she was at the top. The latter loudly clanged on the second floor with each hurried step. Her left hand reached to grab for the lock, but her quick movement knocked it back a foot or so. With a quick shot glance to the right, she could see Ken reach the top of the staircase, looking up at her but not moving. With all her strength she pulled up the entryway staircase and hung onto it, holding the knife between her jaws. She threw herself to her left, picked up the lock, fumbled it onto the chain without locking it, drew the chain through the ring on the floor just beyond the entranceway, and locked it shut.

With three jarring, rattling tugs, Ken yanked on the entranceway door.

"Shit!", she could hear his muffled yell.

—What Now?—

Becky smacked Ken across the head. "Moron!"

"I know, I know." He replied, looking down with an air of confidence that could be called nonexistent.

Sandra stared at them both, looked up to the second floor, then back down to them again. "Becky, that won't do anything. We need to get her out, that's all that matters."

Ken looked to Sandra, "we can just wait her out."

"Or burn her out." Becky grinned.

"No. No one will believe she killed herself by fire. Doesn't make sense. They'll look for someone else. Us." Sandra said, rubbing her chin before snapping her fingers and pointing forcefully at Ken. "Your idea is fine. Even if it takes a few days, we wait her out. We have food down here, water. Up there she has shit."

"But that sounds boring," whined Becky.

"What if someone else comes to rent the place?" Asked Ken.

"You're looking at the next guest," said Sandra. "In three days' time I'll begin my stay and I'll be the witness to something just awful. I sent the request from my phone, got on hers, accepted the request, bing bang boom, this is their tomb."

—

Kristy crawled across the floor of the narrow attic

space. She reached into her right pocket and pulled out her

phone, turning on the flashlight function before scanning the

environment. There were boxes full of Christmas

decorations, even more tools that must not have fit in the

garage, and various scotch tape-sealed boxes.

She pulled herself up a bit to gain a sight advantage

over the box of tools, rummaged through, knocking some

clanging wrenches together before grabbing a rope.

She looked back to the ladder attached to the attic's

entryway door and had an idea. With a lunging motion she

moved towards the ladder, shone her flashlight around until

finding the knife, picked it up, and tied it to the lowest rung of the sliding ladder, reinforcing its strength by bracing the sheath between the lowest rung and the rung just above. She knocked it with her knuckle; no movement.

Now, time to wait. Time to listen to the occasional rumble of dry thunder, each boom interspersed with leaves hitting the sheet metal roof, ostensibly sliding off to a greater pile below.

She checked her phone; no bars. With a sigh, she laid back and put her arms behind her head. She turned and stared into the darkness for a few minutes until a light showed from her phone in her peripheral vision. Even from just the phone, it was enough to illuminate the whole attic. She grabbed the phone, looked, and saw a message from Amazon that her package would be delivered the next day. A sweater she had ordered. With another sigh, she put the phone back down, laid back, and then a flash of recognition hit her. There were two bars!

She grabbed the phone, scrolled down, thinking *tell me I have her number, tell me I have her number.*

She reached "Sandra H. – PTA". She clicked call.

From downstairs she could hear Sandra's phone ring.

"You. What a surprise. I figured we'd have to sweat you out longer."

"Why are you really doing this, Sandra? My family is *dead*, you've already won."

"It's all related, hon', our drives are determined by our experiences."

She could hear Sandra pacing around through the phone.

"I'm not my husband."

"But you let it happen. You stood by, you did nothing, and it happened."

"Oh, Sandra, how disillusioned can you be? You think my life was so perfect?"

"I think it could be worse."

"Well, congratulations, bitch. But, in the end, the differentiation between right and wrong really isn't all that discreet. You crossed a line when you set my son up for death. Deckland, fine, Deckland had it coming...but, Beck."

There was a pause before Sandra replied.

"In the end, justice and silence have nothing to do with one another. You were quiet about your husband, and your precious little Beck would have been no better."

Furious, Kristy almost threw the phone against the attic wall. Instead, she sighed, closed her eyelids with her right index finger and thumb and said, "Fine. Then let me come down and just you and I have it out."

"Gladly."

"But it won't be that simple. I know your idiot daughter and that other doofus will just jump out and slit my throat the second I come down. You, yourself, come up and get me. You alone."

—

After speaking with Becky and Sandra, Ken looked as if he had been told the meaning of life and hadn't liked what he heard. From there, he made his way up the staircase, as opposed to Sandra—as was arranged between the three—slowly.

As he held the railing, about halfway up, he gave the women a cautious glance with a pause in his movement, then continued. Once at the top, he cupped his right hand over his mouth and yelled, "alright, lady! It's just me up here."

No answer, but he heard the rattling of a chain and the sound of a thick, metal piece being thrown down on the thin attic floor.

Still, no answer.

Ken growled, grumbled, and reached for the rope to lower the attic entryway. He did, and just then another rumble of thunder echoed over the mountain. It startled him in unison with the attic entryway door dropping down. With the entryway door came the ladder itself…and with that, the braced knife. The knife lodged its way directly into Ken's left eye. Just as quickly as the ladder's slide, Ken belched out an awful, guttural scream. He put his hand on the sheath of the blade and tried to pull it loose, but it was too tightly lodged between the ladder rungs. As if being held in place by the knife, which he very much was, his posture held rigid but frantic as he first tried to pull himself back slowly. But the pain was too much and he gave up for a moment. Then, with a quick jerk, he yanked himself backwards, escaping the grip of the trap, and entered the grip of death.

Downstairs, Becky had nearly run to him with the first scream, but Sandra held her back, shaking her head. Once they both heard the thump of Ken's body smacking the ground, they slowly moved up single file to the second level. There they saw Ken, the open attic door, the ladder with the knife now piercing the second story's floor, and felt a breeze. The window to the back of the house, the side with the trellis, was open.

Becky bent towards Ken, sobbing while stroking his hair, yet avoiding the ocular wound.

Sandra barely gave Ken a glance. He was of no use anymore. Hardly was of any use before, for that matter.

"Becky," hissed Sandra, "check the attic. What did we talk about? You turn a blind eye. You don't see shit all, you don't say shit all. Now, *go!*"

—

Once she knew that Ken was dead, Kristy bolted

down the ladder wearing only her socks, and threw up the

window. Then, she bolted back up the ladder, went to the

far-left corner of the attic, consumed by darkness, curled up,

and waited. She had a feeling that it wouldn't have been

Sandra that came up to get her. She also figured she

wouldn't send up her own daughter. That left Ken.

Admittedly, she was accurate in her approximation. Still,

Sandra was the one Kristy really wanted. The puppet

master.

Then, a dreadful thought. *What is the point? I'm dead anyway, even if it's only...deep.*

No! No. Beck didn't deserve this. Reba deserved none of this. She's dead because she met me, and I can't leave it that way.

In her thoughts, wrapped deep inside of them, she had not heard Becky and Sandra speaking. However, she did feel the reverberations in the thin attic wood as Becky climbed the ladder.

Once Kristy saw Becky's hair—and knew it wasn't Sandra—she thought, *you killed my son, but I'm better than you. I won't do the same to you.*

She grabbed Becky's hair and smacked her head against the wood, knocking her out cold.

She pulled Becky up, and rolled her out of sight, into the darkness of the attic.

107

From there she descended the staircase, closed it up, and peered out the open window. No sight of Sandra. Her attention whipped to the first story when she heard the bang of the front door.

There she was.

Hastily, Kristy exited the window and began climbing down the trellis. A quarter of the way down, she felt her foot break through the thin plastic, but held steady, breathing hard. Then, slower, she descended. With a quarter left to go, another crack, then a snap. She felt the force as she fell backwards, hitting her head on the pebbles of the walkway below. Her hand moved back behind her head. No severe wound. She got up and began stumbling down the walkway. She had composure, but not as much as she'd care to.

What she needed was a distraction tactic.

Perhaps there'd be a bonfire tonight after all.

She reached in her pocket, but not lighter. It was in the house, on the small foyer table. But Sandra was in there too. *Shit.*

She circled the house and moved her way to the small shed with the sheet metal roof. Gently, she lifted the top. She flashed her glance to her right. The front door was still closed. Good. Her hand moved down into the shed and grabbed the cannister of kerosene. Evenly, yet hurriedly, she poured it all over the circular fire pit. For now, it would have to do. Still, one more step. Really, there were two.

She went back to the rear of the cabin, grabbed a pebble, and threw it into the half open window upstairs. No response from inside. She'd need more to make a stir. She grabbed several pebbles, seven or eight she figured, and

threw them all in. Some smashed the upper portion of the

window, through both panes of glass. Then, she heard

Sandra running upstairs. Kristy remained in place for a bit.

Once she could hear Sandra reach the top of the spiral

staircase, she bolted down the gravely pathway, making

enough noise so she knew Sandra would hear her.

With only her ears assisting her, she heard Sharon

begin her way down the trellis. Fool.

Once Kristy rounded the cabin she burst through the

front door, grabbed the lighter, ran out to the fire pit, and

grabbed a branch out of the pit that had been doused in

kerosene along with the remainder of the wood.

She braced herself. She hugged the cabin's front wall

with her back. Waiting.

Finally, Sandra rounded the corner, now too at the front of the cabin.

With all her might, she elbowed Sandra in the throat then shoved her directly onto the fire pit.

With a sniffle, Sandra looked up and said, "you forgot one important part."

"So did you; smokers never forget a lighter" said Kristy as she lit the doused branch and tossed it down on both Sandra and the pit. Both roared in flames. One roared in screams. At least, for a time. Then, the only sounds were just the owls, crackling from the fire, and another rip of thunder.

–Reprieve–

Kristy felt very little when she saw the rolling red and blues flashing up the hill, brighter and closer. She had had a night. She had broken her own boundaries. While it felt good to be alive, what she felt more was resentment. Not just for the three who had torn her life into shreds, but towards herself. She was a liability. Reba could testify to that, were she able to speak.

She felt the first flicker of hope when Officer Chet Williams parked the car, stumbled out, and stared at the fire. He couldn't help but focus on the legs sticking out.

"What the hell happened here?" He asked, drawing

his service pistol. One must be cautious. Kristy understood

the reaction.

"*You!*" Screamed another voice. It came from

behind Kristy as she made her way to officer Williams with

arms raised. Becky.

Without looking back, Kristy knew that Becky had

stopped in her tracks. Be it having seen her frying mother,

the officer with his weapon raised—now aimed at her—or a

combination of both. Kristy also heard Becky drop a knife

she had grabbed from the kitchen.

From that point forward, Kristy would tell the officer

a story.

Becky would only stare and grin at them both from

the back of the squad car.

Behavior in one's teens can prove to be one hell of an identifier.

"Where is she?" A panicked Officer Williams asked Kristy as he tucked his service weapon into its holster.

"Who?" She asked as she looked over to the squad car, not ten yards away. With some immediacy she recognized it as a stupid question.

"Reba."

Then it occurred to her. She hadn't called 911. He *knew* Reba, that's why he was here in the first place. He must have turned on the squad car's beacon lights when he heard the screaming and the struggle as he pulled up the long, curving driveway.

Kristy led Officer Williams to her best friend's body. A friend she knew for less than a day. When she saw his reaction to Reba, tied up and bloodied, she got the gist of their relationship. Officer Williams sobbed after he held his index and middle finger to her carotid artery, then began untying her.

Any doubt in Officer Williams' mind about Kristy's innocence was erased when he saw her walk up with a similar breaking disposition to his and help him untie his girlfriend.

With his voice shaking, he unhooked his radio and brought it up towards his face. "This is Williams, I need to report a 55-A. Contact Ziereski at the M.E. office and get him here now. If he's not awake, change that."

He pushed his radio back into the clip above his left breast plate. He looked up to Kristy. They both said nothing until Officer Williams led her out of Reba's house and down the path towards the squad car.

"Can you give us a statement this evening, Ms...."

Kristy just nodded and wiped away a tear.

Then, she loaded herself into the front seat of the squad car. Becky stared at the back of her head from the back seat. It ended up being a quiet ride to the station.

Kristy never did get the last of her cigarettes. She didn't even think about them.

Stone Souls

–A Man Torn Asunder–

I stood there looking at a gravestone that now served as the resting place for two bodies. A kid, in his teens, smashed against it. Now, his body was lying on the ground. Only his head touched the stone. About a foot above, a circular crack mark, like rings on a horrid tree stump.

I hadn't resided in Crockett long enough to know the town and its occupants front to back and back to front. But, even if I were to have been a long time resident, this kid's face was too smashed to even identify. His cheek bones were flattened, nose bent all the way to the left. His closed eyes faced the heavens, darkened and cloudy now. The sun struggled to break through, ready for dawn. A storm, with a fog bank intertwined, was rolling in. I wanted this done. Not only because of the storm but, for the first time on this job, my stomach was churning.

Just how this occurred, yet to be determined; identity, a mystery. To leave the blood smeared across the tombstone the way it was. It was as if this kid were thrown like a baseball. Whoever did it did not seem like a player in the minor league, either.

My gut told me to use 55-A, homicide, when I called back into the station. Nothing about this seemed accidental. I turned and pulled my radio from my duty belt. "Dispatch this is J.B., come in, over."

"J.B. this is dispatch." A woman's voice came through static over his radio. Cristin, the dispatcher who would answer nine times out of ten. Her answer was always predictable. She loved herself some overtime and, after all, she was only one of two dispatchers.

"Responding to 10-59. If there was mischievous behavior, it's ended. This is a 10-70..."

I had become used to using codes over the radio. Though, truth be told, they were becoming antiquated with time. But, in a small town, antiquated is just another term for homely. "...homicide. We need to get a M.E. here now. Storm's coming in and there are details to comb."

"Medical Examiner Weiss said she will be there in five." She said.

Quick, and par for the course in that. Our station was efficient because it had no choice but to be. With a town population as comparably miniscule as ours, sometimes it seemed even a stolen candy bar would set the alarm bells

ringing.

"Roger. Over and out," I said and put my radio back

in its holster. A rippling blast of thunder startled me. It was

either the electricity in the air's moisture or my nerves that

sent my arm hairs up like they were saluting a superior

officer.

For the first time in a long time, I felt truly alone on a

case. Ironic, considering I had always requested just that. I

suppose I've always figured myself a real-life Dirty Harry,

pardon the cliche. Years of that gets to you, especially when

the world keeps getting more violent and producing stuff

like this. I couldn't tell for sure, but the kid looked fifteen.

No older than my boy was at the time. That was why...I just

felt sure he was about fifteen.

A single droplet of rain, carried by the wind from miles off, struck my forehead. As it slid down my forehead, I wiped it from my brow and twisted my feet in the mud. It must have rained at some point in the night. I assumed because, while I lived only a few miles from that graveyard, I saw or heard no rain. It must have been brief, and somewhat restrained to this secluded area.

But *this* restrained? It must have been the most confined rain storm of the century.

From behind me, a jarring screeching sound that accompanied the opening of the gate leading into the graveyard. The grave digger and sexton, Matthias. Tall fellow, taller than me and I stand over six feet.

"Hey Sergeant Blum, I had to go and lock up. Once I saw..." Matthias flipped his gaze to the body.

"Yeah," I said as I lit a cigarette. I let it hang from my mouth as I continued speaking, "it's incredible…and sick." My shaking hand jostled my cigarette so hard ash flew about. A chunk landed on my crisp, leather patrol boot. At least, at one point it was crisp. Now, it was caked in mud, most likely ruined were it not designed to take that and more.

Matthias looked to me with a look of fear coupled with genuine concern on his face.

"Unacceptable in this town." I said as I put the cigarette back in my mouth and looked back down at the young man.

"Yeah. Well, last night—early this morning I guess— I saw these kids out here hollering and drinking, heard some music," Matthias said as he looked to me. "The town of

Crockett is above this sort of thing happening to anyone. It is above serious crimes. They do *not* happen here. Most of all, it is above citizens feeling fear that something like this *could* happen that would disrupt their lives in an instant." Matthias snapped his fingers. "Point being, these kids weren't supposed to be here."

Was he using a tone with me?

I paused as I pointed down to the young man. "It is my job to ensure that be the truth; about the town being safe. Not just for myself, but for everyone, including this kid laying on the ground, regardless of whether he was meant to be here or not." I snapped back. My ex always said I snapped when I felt failure. That must have been what this crime scene was to me, a failure. Even if he was angry with me, I at least somewhat understood. I've received negative reactions while on duty from just about everyone I meet.

Why should Matthias be any different?

Matthias only nodded in reply. With that being said, he looked like he realized he was over-externalizing his fear and misdirecting it to me. At least, that was my theory.

I knew this situation was unusual. For whatever reason, though, I didn't even question whether or not it was drug related. As much as the presumed age of the boy inspired that thought process, there were no devices, residue. No real signs of drug use anywhere.

I heard something from behind me. Metal, moving around.

I turned. Nothing. No other presence, save for Matthias. He looked confused. Had he heard nothing? Was this just me?

"You okay, Sergeant Blum?" He asked.

I waved him off as I walked past the body and down the hill, a gut feeling. I stopped as a *clank* rang out across the foggy graveyard. I flipped through my belt, padding the objects until I reached my flashlight. The light barely broke through the increasing fog. It hit a separate gravestone. Though this one was undamaged, thank God. It read 'Larry Ballast', a recently deceased local. I had heard the name.

The hill appeared to have rolled an empty soda can right into Larry's gravestone. No, not a soda can, a spray paint can. It had hit the stone hard enough to spray red paint up and all over it. The can spewed and hissed until all that remained was air. I couldn't touch it, it would contaminate the scene, but even through the thick fog I could see the label, 'Krylon Industrial', the strong stuff. Kid must have gotten it from our hardware store, or out of town.

126

Precious few businesses in town had a wide enough inventory to carry even that.

"What do you have down there, J.B?" Matthias's baritone yet frantic voice cut through the encroaching fog over the hill. Enough to scare me upright. 'The Willies', that's what my boy always said. No clue where he got it from.

"Questions." I said to myself as I looked down at the can. No paint anywhere, *any*where except what sprayed up on Larry's gravestone. But, as far as actually pulling the nozzle and painting…none. Second thoughts or somebody stopped him, perhaps both.

Matthias?

"Huh?" His voice rang again.

Did I say that out loud?

127

"What?" I called out.

"What was it you said?"

"Uh, nothing. It's nothing." I said as I began to make my way up the hill.

"Nothing down there?" He asked as I leaned against the gravestone of the boy. The fog was thick enough now to the point I could barely see Matthias. Just his green eyes. Green eyes always shimmer, more than the rest, at least to me. There was something else in his eyes, though. Nerves.

"You alright, Matt? You look nervous." I asked.

"Matthias, please." He said with a smile.

"Gift from God, right?" I asked.

"Mm-hmm, yep. That's what it means." He jittered about and asked, "You ready to see the other two?"

"Three total?" I asked, surprised and perhaps a bit too forcefully. This came as a surprise, though. I wasn't at the station when we got the call from Matthias about the vagrants tearing up his property.

Could have been three, could have been two, truth be told I hardly remembered. In all honesty, I hadn't gotten to looking for another body. I just couldn't help staring at the boy…or what was left of him. Anyway, when dispatch called me the radio was nothing if not static. Day after day of overnight shifts to take out the trash before the holidays. Literally, not in a way of 'taking out the trash', an unfortunate expression I had heard people use before to refer to other human life. We don't seem to give a damn until problems are right in our face, when the problem is subjectively important to us. That's why I moved here, amongst other reasons, from the city. I got sick of the consistent malicious asides and attitudes. Sad thing is, all told, they were the best part of the job when you consider the genuinely insane things I had seen people *do* to one another. Apparently, this town of Crockett wasn't so different at all. It just needed time to show its true colors.

"Yes, Sergeant Blum. Again, when I called several hours ago, I said there were a few kids tearing around here. Y'all really need to step it up. Have you just seen the one body?"

So, yes, he was using a tone with me.

The way he asked me with a perturbed nature I found to be a catalyst for my own perturbed nature. Each could exacerbate the other, so I decided to continue professionally. Not to mention, he had a point, I hadn't even looked for the other body. Hadn't occurred to me. Just seeing that one kid's face…it threw me. I never expected

this from Crockett.

II – Be Careful About Influence

"Would you just hurry up?" Terri Papas barked at

her brother, Rod, from the front of the line of four. Terri

stood about five feet tall with brown hair tied into a bun.

She was followed by Rhodes, or 'Rod', then Paul and

Bartholomew Weiss as they made their way down a rocky

path. Pebbles skirted from beneath their feet and clacked to

one another. Aside from the blue hue of the moon, it was

pitch black out on the path. No street lights, just trees and

varied wildlife singing about their collective evenings.

Bartholomew towered over his brother, and pulled

him in close by the shoulder. "Thanks for coming out, man.

I appreciate it. I think Terri does too," he said with a

knowing smile as he looked down to his brother. He found it a valid enough attempt to boost his little brother's confidence, joke or not.

"What? No." Paul replied.

"Oh, I don't know, kid. Think she might." He smiled again as he looked up towards Terri and Rod. "How much further, you two?" He yelled

Paul waved backwards, as if to say 'we'll get there when we get there'. Bart sighed and looked back down to his brother before saying, "shouldn't be too much longer."

Lightning crackled, and thunder roared. Paul jumped what must have been nearly three feet in the air. His brother grabbed him and pulled him in close. "It's okay," he said.

"Mom wouldn't want us at the graveyard." Paul said with what Bart perceived as welling tears.

"She wants you to get out of the house. That's what we've both wanted for you, kid." Bart tilted his head, a clear attempt to be supportive and understanding.

Despite being ten years younger, with a not quite fully developed brain or personality, Paul understood this. He knew his brother cared for him deeply, but also that he couldn't replace their father. Had Paul been a bit older, his brother's empathic response would have most likely led him to believe the truth…that his brother, too, was hurting. "Well, I don't like these two!" He yelled. Bart rushed him, grabbed his shoulder and *hushed* him. Terri and Rod looked back. Embarrassed, Bart gave them a smile to convey apology, and gave his brother a stern look

"I'm sorry, Bart," Paul whispered, "I don't know them though."

"I know, neither do I really. But, look, if we're going to start up a new life somewhere else we need to at least make an effort and practice here, where it'll be easier, right? Home field advantage?" Bart parented.

"I guess," Paul said as he tripped over a rock. They were getting bigger as they neared the curve to reach the graveyard, imperceptible behind a thicket of trees.

Bart caught him and rubbed his back. "You good?"

"Yeah, thanks." Paul shot his brother a look, and Bart removed his hand from his brother's shoulder. "I've got it." Paul said after a beat.

"Young, smart and full of heart." Bart said as he looked down what little of the pathway there was remaining.

Just up ahead, as they bent the curve, was a small church house, white with blue shudders. Rustic, classic, and miniscule.

"Used to be a school, back in the day." Rod said as he slowed to match pace with the brothers; Terri further up ahead. "My Mom said it used to be that this was the only school. So, like, twenty people must have lived here. Now there's just one guy who lives there now."

"Can we go in?" Paul asked as he stared to the church house. "I'd like to see it."

"Nope. Locked. Always." Rod said in a hurry with a loud whisper. "Behind it, though, is the graveyard." He held up a can of spray paint. "And that's where we're

going. See it? Through the fog?"

Bart and Paul both put their right hands up to their

head, as if saluting. Both looked to the other and chuckled

for the sake of synchronicity as well as the fact that shielding

one's eyes to see only works if the sun is the main

obstruction. Fog? Not so effective.

They approached the gate and wedged their way

through. The bottom of the chain link gate scraped into the

mud until it couldn't budge any further. Once they were

through, they started carefully trudging through the mud.

Suddenly, a startling clang from behind them. The gate had

an easier time closing than opening. The brothers shook it

off and kept moving.

In front of them, a sign read "Mountain Memorial Graveyard'. The size of the graveyard was moderate in comparison to ones in bigger towns; what few other towns Bart and Paul had visited. Like all other graveyards, it contained history nonetheless.

"Watch out for the hill," Bart said to Paul as he pointed just beyond a line of gravestones. Down the hill, there were positioned rows of even more gravestones before a final eastern fence line.

Paul wandered around the graveyard, rubbing his hand on stone after stone as he made his way towards the north side and laid his hands atop the fence. One prong created an ever so slight incision on his right palm. A small amount of blood rolled over the lines on his hand, with some of it making its way down the line and the rest pooling over and falling to the ground. Then, it began sliding down the grass and making its way into the soil.

"You alright?" Bart's voice startled Paul from behind as he stared at his palm.

"Yes. God, stop asking." Paul said as Bart nodded three times, put his hands in his pockets, defeated, and made his way over to Terri and Rod.

Terri raised her eyebrow, "what's up?"

"Nothing," Bart said. "He's just scared, I think."

"Huh. Well, there's really only one cop in this town. And he's new. So, we're good." Terri replied and shot him what he figured to be an attempt at a reassuring expression.

"Guys, I'm not sure he's even thinking about the police. Maybe this was a bad idea, maybe he's scared of this place." Bart said and looked to the ground for a few moments before he looked back up. Were Terri and Rod

more sensitive people, he would have seen a look of at least

moderate concern on their faces. He did not, and found that

unsettling.

Rod began shaking a red paint can, and Terri a

yellow. They shook them for what seemed like minutes to

the nervous Bart. "Guys, I really don't think—"

"We're not hurting anybody. Grab a can," Rod

snapped. As they left his presence, he could hear Rod

whisper, "Shouldn't have invited him. I told him not to

bring his stupid brother."

Terri made her way to the west gate, Rod towards

the center, towards a huge, stone statue. Once all the way to

the west gate, Terri lifted herself on top of a three-foot tall,

curved gravestone and hobbled, holding her arms out to her

140

sides. She then leapt to another and felt she had stability for only the briefest moment before she felt her heel jerk. She avoided smashing her sternum against the stone, instead smacking her left shoulder against it.

Bart could see her head poke out from behind the gravestone before she lifted herself again and, with somehow remaining confidence free ran across four more standard curved stones. He looked on to Rod, just walking around with his paint can aimed, but not spraying. Then, his gaze ascended the statue. The subject didn't look familiar, perhaps just a local Crockett hero of sorts. He noticed a second statue up towards the north side, where Paul remained holding the fence. He turned back to the way they came, the south. No one was coming. As far as he was concerned, that was very good.

He looked back up to the center statue, somewhat more confident that his brother was fine. The eyes of the statue looked off into the distance, though he could swear that they met his gaze. If even for just a brief moment.

We're not hurting anybody, Rod says. It'll all be fine, Rod says.

He looked back to his brother. "Well, we might be hurting him," Bart mumbled to himself as he bent down and rummaged through the plastic shopping bag. Now only one paint can remained; another red. He picked it up and gave it three shakes. The liquid sloshed left and right, left and right, left and— an abrupt *thump*. Bart looked down to the can with a raised brow, then looked back up to his brother. Now, neither he nor the gate he leaned on could be seen through the fog. But, now, not even the statue at the north side appeared either. Even with the fog, it should have towered over enough to be visible. He made his way over to where his brother once stood, using his palm to feel out impending stones and other such obstructions.

"What is-? Where is-?" Bart stammered. A much louder thump now, enough to turn his attention to the west gate. No Terri now either. The fog had concealed just about everything around him with the exception of a five plus foot circumference. It surrounded him like a wall until Rod soared by, slicing the wispy fog, smashing into a gravestone just above the hill. The red spray can fell from his hand and sat loosely on a pile of grass, just to the initial decline of the hill.

Even with the lull in the fog's density, Bart could barely tell what broke through the fog after Rod. It looked like just a gray blob. Tall, thick, heavy. The ground shook beneath his feet and, more than ever before in his life, he felt

143

the cold, piercing tug of fear. More than when his Father fell

ill. More than when his Mother told Paul and himself that

they would soon be leaving Crockett to move in with family

out West. After all, every town and city needs a coroner

service. This was the first time in the three intermediate

days after she had dropped that bomb that he didn't worry

about Paul's emotional health. Now, the sinking feeling of a

judgment lapse fell on Bart. They should have been side by

side. All the way. Like he promised.

"Paul! Paul, Paul! Where are you man? Come on!

Where are ya bud we need to go!" Bart twisted in panic,

staring around himself as the heavy footsteps rumbled

again. Now they were closer as a gray form brushed by him,

sending him tumbling.

Mud wedged itself in his eyes as he flopped to the

ground. He rubbed his index fingers over his eyelids,

wiping away just enough mud to see a figure standing over Rod. It slammed him to the concrete gravestone, forehead first. It lifted Rod, now nearly unconscious with eyes closed down to a weak sliver. He lifted the spray paint and began to spew paint over the figure's face. Whatever it was, Bart knew it was huge. Teen feet tall, maybe more, because Rod was hovering in the air and spraying upwards. Trace amounts of red paint sprayed through the fog and caught Bart's hair before the figure grabbed Rod's head and smashed him against the gravestone one final time.

The figure turned, and stood still, facing west. *Does it not see me?* Bart thought as he turned his head left and stared west as well. Nothing, just more and more fog. However, enough fog had dissipated that, it appeared at least, the center statue also was gone.

His mind raced trying to find a logical explanation, but there wasn't one to be found. It was the statue, moving, walking.

Impossible. This is impossible. Wake up. Wake up. WAKE! UPPPP!

The statue turned both its feet in unison, facing Bart directly as Terri's screams rang across the graveyard, until a very sudden stop, mid-scream. Like an old car engine hacking its last breath. The only thing Bart felt—save for fear—was confusion. Then, the fog began to rise all at once. The abrupt and bizarre rise of the fog scared Bart nearly as much as seeing the clear sight of Rod's body laying against the grave stone. Blood, or paint, was splotched against the concrete slab. Bart figured it was a combination of both as he stared back to the spray paint in his hand.

Without warning, the statue lurched towards him and picked him up by the shirt on his back. It slammed him down on the ground. "Young!" Bart yelled in a state of apparent disorientation. It slammed him again. "Smart!" He yelled. The statue held Bart in the air as Paul brushed through the fog, it finally having risen to provide clarity for him to try and find his brother.

C'mon, kid. Run.

His little brother must have had a similar idea, because he ran back and slid behind a tall gravestone before the statue saw him.

"Full of heart," Bart said as he looked to his brother's face, peaking over from behind the stone to the north.

The look of terror across his brother's face made Bart feel a profound sense of failure, and an even more profound sense of helplessness. With what little energy he could muster, he dropped the spray paint, as if he had forgotten he still held it, and held his right index finger up to his lips as the statue slammed him down to the mud one final time. A crunching noise reached Paul's ears as he stared at his brother, laying on the ground with his finger still up to his mouth. The statue that stood above Bart looked down to its prey emotionless and stagnant. Then, it stepped on his body and slowly pushed. The squishing of the mud and the general horridness of the situation confused Paul as to whether he should cover his eyes, his ears, or both. Though, young as he was, he knew he should do neither. He had to move and he had to move now while the statue was distracted.

With the opportunity provided, Paul rushed behind a tall stretch of gravestones surrounded by a thicket of bushes, a little further towards the pedestal for the north east statue. He placed his hand over one knee, then the other, and held himself close, shivering. The statue from the center entered its rightful place once again with a stomp and then concrete sliding against concrete until…silence. Light rain fell, solely on the statue as if it were walled by sprinklers, washing the paint from its face down into the soil.

Paul sat, hyperventilating as the statue from the north east corner lumbered over him. He held the spray can in his hand, staring into the stone eyes of the statue. He threw it, sending it hurdling and clanging against the gate. He held his arms up as if to say *See? No threat.* The statue turned and with rigid posture moved towards its pedestal, braced itself with a hand on the podium as it climbed, and then stood motionless.

III – Next Steps

I reached the other body, to the western side of the graveyard. Matthias stood behind me, arms crossed as I examined body number two. Female, young; about the same age as the unidentified male leaning against the gravestone. Unlike him, though, her eyes were wide open. What once housed pupils and retinas now housed only slivers of stone, as if they were perfectly placed on her eyes. These, though, they *were* her eyes. Solid, facing north. A chilling sight.

Never had I seen anything like that and Matthias must have noticed, especially when I just about leapt back and ran into him. He patted my shoulder and asked, "are you okay, Sergeant?"

"Yeah," I said as I looked to the distance through the fog to see a yellow rotating light. As it reached closer, I could see it was attached to a vehicle, a hearse. A woman exited and made her way towards us before stopping short, turning around to reach into her vehicle and switch off the lights.

"Gentlemen," she said with a steep serving of stoicism. "What have we got this morning? Outside of fog."

"Three bodies," I said as I pointed to the female to the west, the male to the east and then to the body at the center. The boy lay on the ground, even with a burly figure he was clearly overtaken, perhaps even pushed down into the chunk of earth that now surrounded his body. "Are you alright, miss? You look a little worse for wear."

I regretted my words immediately, still she only smiled them off, somehow creating even more bags under her eyes. "My kids never came home last night. God must know where they are because I sure do not. When they get home...anyway, let me see the bodies."

"Sure," I said as I led her to the young woman.

"Blunt force trauma," she said as she slipped on her gloves. "Can tell you that from standing over here." She bent down and examined the wound on the girl's head.

"Same for the other two." I said and looked to her. Her eyes flashed surprise as she rose. "Four total here last night, right Matthias?" I asked.

"Yes sir, ah, and ma'am; there were four, total. At least I'm almost positive I heard four voices. Only seen three bodies so far, though. Didn't even know they were bodies until just before he showed up." Matthias said to her. "Sorry, I didn't catch your name," he finished as he extended his right hand.

She met him with a hand of her own and shook. "Crystal Weiss, M.E."

"Matthias Albricht, gravedigger." He paused, "That doesn't sound as good as M.E."

"No, but it is a line." She said, meaning line of work.

I knew she meant 'line of work'. Matthias must have taken it as a discarding statement, and left the two of us to continue our work, making his way back up to his little church house. "I'll tell you what, seeing all this has made me less inclined to sleep at night. Going to head back up to the house. Sergeant, I assume you're coming by later with more questions?"

"Uh, yes, most likely." I said, stating the truth as best I could understand it. There were too many questions to have answered before I could ask him any more of my own.

Crystal looked up to him and said, "Goodbye," before turning back to me. "Oh, Mr. Albricht."

Matthias turned around. "Ma'am?"

"Why didn't you investigate for yourself? If you thought they were just kids on your property why not confront them?"

"Because what woke me up was the screaming."
Matthias tucked his hands into his coat pockets and resumed walking.

Crystal turned to me and shrugged. "Now, sergeant, I can tell you right now that's Terri Papas. Local kid, of course. She and her brother start up something to irritate the town every now and again. Never quite like this, though, obviously. Point being, they were usually quite harmless, though annoying." She walked to the east and approached the boy leaning against the gravestone, "and, now, while I can't quite tell who this is, I guarantee you this'd be the brother, Rhodes. Kids in town call him Rod."

She used her right gloved hand to wipe a few strands of hair from the boy's forehead. "Blunt force trauma as well. Whoever did this is *very* large. Christ, must be huge."

155

I felt inclined to agree with her. I fancy myself somewhat larger in stature than other Crockett residents, but there's no way I could have done what was done there that morning. It would have had to be someone, perhaps, even twice as strong as myself. Especially when it came to the third victim, towards the center of the graveyard. We made our way over to him, down in the dirt with head tilted ever so slightly left, index finger placed against his lips.

"Looks like rigor mortis set in," I said as I bent down to face the boy. "Odd position, though." I used a pencil to move the boy's finger with precision and caution. It moved, with just a slight wriggle. "And it couldn't have been any longer than two hours, either. Hasn't fully set in yet."

The fog, however, *had* set in and it was enough to distort our vision.

Once she had moved in closer, Crystal had a brief look of confusion, then recognition. Her mouth widened and she stepped back. "That shirt. That's..." She turned and vomited against one of the gravestones. Embarrassed, perhaps, she placed her hand over her mouth and composed herself enough to reexamine the body. Her head bobbed up and down as she said through broken voice and welling tears, "That's my son."

Never had I experienced an incident where a fellow officer on the scene, or in this case a medical examiner, had known the victim. Years in the city, so much crime, I always figured I would. Prepared for it even. I've seen enough educational videos on protocol for dealing with shock victims. Here, though, her movements were exacting. Grief affects us in different ways, but she was running like mad around the graveyard. Yet, she wasn't just frantic. It was as if she were trying to get on top of the situation. Like always, I figured. Must be a single parent. "Paul! Paul! If you are here, this is your Mother. Where are you?!" She gave off a piercing scream.

She rushed back to the center and bent down to touch her son's face, rubbing his cheek as she attempted to pull his extended finger away from his lips. From behind a gravestone to the northeast, a hissing sound reached the two.

"What was that?" I asked, in all actuality, to no one in particular.

Crystal remained bent over, knees in the mud, attempting to get a hold on her son's flattened body. Through her sobbing, I could swear I heard light pouting, though from a different source. Somewhere close to where paint was now spraying up on the fence. As I approached the chain links, I could see a can with a small incision, spewing up air and paint. A whimper caught my attention, and I reached through the fog to feel…hair?

A boy leapt up and smacked me in the mouth, sending me tumbling back against the fence. I have no problem admitting it scared me a little more than half to death.

"Paul!" Crystal screamed and leapt from the center boy's body, rushing to her other son and lifting him from the ground before giving him a bear hug. "Oh, what happened? What happened, baby?"

The boy stared at me, emotionless, chin resting on his Mother's left shoulder. Looking into his eyes was enough to tell me there was one hell of a story here. They also were enough to tell me I'd probably never hear it, nor would anyone. Unlike the remainder of the graveyard, his eyes still contained love, fear, empathy…all the qualities that make a person a person. But, he, well he wasn't all the way there. At least not for now.

My concern was alleviated as the boy pushed his head down to his mother's shoulder and cried. A measure that she returned. I walked away, out of the gate, as the two embraced. They needed their space, and I had something to do.

I walked to my squad car and bent down to the passenger seat, removing my cell phone. It was one of those old flip phones, and because of its age it now had a strange affectation where no matter what, the buttons blurted out a tone with each button press, even when the phone itself should be silenced. I held the phone to my ear and waited through ring after ring.

Maybe too early.

I decided to leave a message: "Hey…baby, it's me. Listen, I'd like to come home. I miss you all. Please, just once, call me back."

With that I flipped the phone shut, threw it back in my car and looked to the mother and son. Despite all the horrible, horrible things the two of them had witnessed…they held one another. And, in that moment, for the two of them it seemed to be enough. For that, I felt thankful.

Maybe too late.

Erosion

I – Sea Sick, Hurry Quick

"So, why is it called Matchstick Island, again?" Billy Reynolds asked his sister. She noticed he had a gleam in his eye that was caused not just by excitement but also by the glimmer of the sun reflecting from them as he looked up to her. Suzanne Reynolds had been lost in thought. For years her life had felt like she had been lost, not in thought, but lost at sea. Perhaps a bit of both. Drifting like an aimless balloon hovering at greater and greater altitudes until one day…*Pop! *

But this trip…this trip was all or nothing. It had to work out. By the end of this she hoped she had the same gleam in her eye as her brother. Not quite likely.

"That's not what it's *really* called. It's like a...a playful pet name, I suppose." She replied as she looked out to the water off the boat's port side. She jotted her eyes down to her brother then back up. Were it not for the heaviness on her heart, she would have been happy to truly notice and take stock of the uptick in her brother's disposition. Her eyes barely matched his before flickering back to the expansive bay. She kept them focused, attempting to pierce the thin wall of mist that sat puffed yet rigid up ahead. Her squint grew more and more narrow. The results were still blurry, as her dwindling eyesight did her few favors. Degenerative, just a matter of time.

Just a matter of time, she thought. She had never remembered the trip taking more than an hour and a half when she had visited the island as a girl. Many times. Many, many times she had been on this ferry. The one ferry to "Matchstick Island" from the shore. Family owned. In fact, *her* family owned it. But not just the Reynolds. The Bracketts, the other prominent family on Matchstick Island, had an equal hand in ensuring the island's financial prosperity. They held a monopoly on the transportation side of the tourist community, while the Reynolds controlled the main attraction: Crab Cakes.

Try as they might, the Bracketts never quite could crack that recipe. And the Reynolds, well, the Reynolds would be damned before parting with it. Member after member of the lineup had perished with the recipe collection finely ingrained within the confines of their skulls.

"A pet name?" He asked.

Suzanne's mind had wandered again, as it had been frequently since her mother's demise. Though, in many ways, it felt like her mother had been dead for months, not just two weeks. Stress will do that to you.

"Uh, yeah, like a term of endearment. Are you familiar with that phrase? No, probably not. It's something that we call a person, place that means something to us. They call it that because, over time, it's become slender and straight, like a matchstick." She held her two index fingers out, one before the other, forming an imaginary, straight line. "It's called erosion. Over time, the land is just...shrinking. Sinking, really. You take sea level rise and storms, mix 'em up, and you've got erosion. Eat your heart out global warming disbelievers."

"What, Suzie?"

"Uh, nothing."

Suzanne rubbed Billy's back and said, "scary thing is, it'd only take one big storm to wipe the place off the map. Won't happen while we're here, but pretty scary, right?

"Yeah, I guess so. You sure it won't happen while we're here?"

"Positive," she replied with a comforting wink and smile.

Her vision caught the briefest flash within the sopping and hazy vista. Then, nothing. Then, again. A yellow light. She figured it was the strobe light that sat on top of the lighthouse. At this distance a mere dot within a foggy landscape.

Then, another flash in her peripheral. She found herself distracted by the glimmer of the rippling water below. Bumpy wave after bumpy wave shown a light resembling a rainbow, as if skipping off the waves. The image as a whole appeared like an unfocused yet beautiful waving flag.

All in all, her eyesight had done her few favors in recent years. Macular degeneration, the doctor had said. Her retina would deteriorate and, the more it did, the more everything would look just like the waves looked now. Thicker and thicker prescriptions were being doled out like hotcakes. On this trip, though, on the ferry, she could swear her vision was just ever so slightly crisper. In fact, physically, she felt pretty well all around. It helped that they were surrounded by calm waters. No nausea on this ride. As far as seeing the island was concerned, the sky was doing them favors. No real sign of a dreaded island-wiping storm like she had described to her brother.

Good, she thought, that was not a conversation she wanted to have with her brother. As far as she was concerned, he possessed a somewhat frightful disposition to begin with. It'd be for the best to keep it that way throughout this trip. No extra stressors.

The fog began to dissipate, and a visible dot within the haze was on its way to formulating into a coherent image.

She figured the little dot must be the island. The bay wasn't known for being crowded to begin with. In fact, for miles and miles, 'Matchstick' sat alone.

"Oh, we—" Billy started before the blare of the boat's roaring horn. His feet hopped from the ground like a young rabbit just learning to use its hinders. They landed on the steel deck of the boat's bow to a ringing clang.

169

"It's okay. That just means we're close." She said.

The little black dot down the shoreline had now nearly formed into the comforting sight of the island. There were vague outlines of buildings, other boats within the water, and a taller structure. In spite of her squinting, even the larger structure would not truly be discernible had she not already been acquainted with the island. It was Matchstick Island's own water tower, a sight she had taken in and appreciated many times as a little girl. Its spinning, yellow strobe light now entered then exited, entered then exited, the vision of the boat's passengers.

Billy seemed particularly enamored by the light, as his head turned to follow it each revolution.

"Is that it?" Billy asked.

Suzanne held her right hand over her eyes, shielding her vision from the sunlight that was beginning to eat its way through the dissipating fog and said, "must be. Nothing else out here I don't think."

The rainbow illusion amongst the rippling waves grew stronger as the clouds broke and the sunlight finally peaked through in full. The foredeck the siblings stood on became illuminated, as if being under a direct spotlight. It was like they were about to be pulled up into the heavens.

Billy ran his hand up the bulkhead railing encompassing the mid-sized ferry as he moved from the port side of the bow to the forefront to gain a better view. It felt cold, icy with the accumulated dew from the most recent storm. It pooled in his hand, lining itself within the crevices before streaming down. He wagged and waved it, sending the remaining beads into the ocean beneath, mixing with the salty water, now like a bobbing head in a New York crowd.

He began to rush back toward the port walkway, with Suzanne's eyes locked on.

"Hey, kiddo." Suzanne asked. Billy spun around and gave her a confused look. "Where ya goin'?"

"Back to the room where—" he started saying.

"-Cabin." She interrupted.

"Cabin. I want to get my game. My stuff."

Suzanne made her way over to Billy and gently grabbed his shoulders. "Bud, we're not here to play the Gameboy or whatever. Anyway, we don't need to be the first to grab our stuff. It's all in a pile, regardless. Patience. Go in there now and everything will fall over."

The main cabin of the ferry housed what amounted to a slender closet for the passengers to stow their collective items. The extent of its organization was that it was entirely disorganized with each and every trip across the bay. This was born of special necessity more than poor craftmanship. Bag upon bag was stuffed in, some cattycornered but not enough to push open the single bolt door that appeared to have been there since the beginning of time. To obtain one's belongings, one first had to obtain permission from the cabin grounded employee, also the soda-serving bartender, as it were. To pull out one bag would lead to chaos. This matter of simple physics seemed to allude each group of passengers.

Time and time again the soda-server would be able to time just when Humpty Dumpty would fall off of that wall. It was when random passenger number one would reach downwards.

The aforementioned executor of the pitiful dinette found this more interesting than flexing their salesmanship muscle with: "Hi! Will that be Sprite, Coke or Oyster Crackers?", "Hello, will that be Sprite, Coke or Oyster Crackers?", "Sprite, Coke or Oyster Crackers?", "Alright, whatcha want?"

"Why *are* we here, Suzie?" He asked.

She could see he was confused and a wave of guilt rushed over her. Even if he was her brother, she only partially saw him as such. Really, she saw herself more as doting mother than patient yet stern sister. She imagined his perception of herself fell more on the latter half of that equation.

174

Even before it all happened, though, she found

herself more the maternal part. There were missed evenings

with friends, missed dates, even a missed spring break. The

latter of which she felt more than comfortable with. She felt

most spring breaks are like an STD scavenger hunt on

Miami Beach.

It had been a big change, first their father ostensibly

running off to Alaska, at least according to their mother,

who had retreated to the island a year ago. It was there she

died. Its residents the people who had not informed the

children of the deceased until after the service was held.

That was the call: 'Hey your Mom's dead, service was nice,

she left a letter for you to read in lieu of her last will and

testament. Come talk to me, the executor of her estate, thank

you very much'. That is what Suzanne retained, at least. If

one were being honest, the call was too short and jarring to be fully remembered.

"Look, it's not for you to worry about. Mom's lawyer is here and…it's a will reading. Okay?" Suzanne assuaged her brother.

She had been told something about this will reading being different. There were stipulations. For one, their father was not allowed on the premises. His presence would negate the reception of anything from the reading. That's what she figured she heard. Because, what she really thought she heard, was that he couldn't be mentioned while on the island. Though, that had to have been ill-advised sarcasm.

For two, the will reading was not just regarding their mother's possessions. Something about bloodlines, the lawyer had said on the phone. She could hardly tell half of what he was saying. The reception on the island was always a nightmare. As far as audible perception went, the islanders' accents were a nightmare as well.

"Why do we have to do it?" He asked.

"Hear the will reading?"

"Yeah."

"Well, because, uh, when someone di-..."

Buuuurrrooooo

The boat roared with an echoing horn honk. It's second, loudest, and last prior to arrival. Startled, both Suzanne and Billy twitched with a jump and looked up to the crisp metallic foghorn. Usually when a vessel emits such a noise, it is to warn of impending hazards. In this case, it was more of a custom. It allowed the islanders to know that

177

more tourists were arriving. It also served to establish some class in the proceedings of taking the old, mostly unattended to ferry across the channel. Tourists were fans of the addition: 'Oh, honey, how neat!', they'd chime. Residents along the channel, in their multi-million-dollar homes – not so much.

It was a quick installation after 'Matchstick' was graciously labelled by National Geographic as one of the top twenty spots to visit in the entire country a few years back. The residents initially embraced it with a sincere 'oh, great' sensibility, which divulged over time to a sarcastic variation of said sensibility.

The ferry was approaching the dock, nearing the end of the voyage. The jagged chine to the bow of the ferry began bisecting impending current at a decreased rate. The waters surrounding the vessel calmed, yielding the result of breathless tranquility.

"…When someone passes," she continued, "they still have stuff here, right? Like, on Earth."

"Okay." She could tell that he had not truly faced their mother's mortality, nor her swift exit from their lives.

At least she left them a house to tag along with the zero explanation, this was a near mantra for Suzanne by this point.

She huffed, exasperated. This conversation wasn't easy for someone in their late twenties such as herself. For a six-year-old, it was a fairly substantial increase in difficulty. Mortality is a tricky thing to educate someone in their single digits about.

"Well, what's been done so far is I've become your guardian. Like, legally."

"Like Mom?"

"Uh, yeah." Suzanne said after a beat.

"And because Dad…"

To the port and starboard sides sat lines of Mid-Channel Buoys. Orange lights, shaped and sized like tennis balls, spun, though it was too light out for the orange to show on the water. Despite the calm nature of the water, somewhat common for the channel, the buoys shook. Softly for a moment, then rough, then soft again before halting to a stop, as if they were sitting motionless on land for a few seconds. Then, they regained their normal bobbing.

"Yes, because Dad." She worried she had cut him off. No, he just couldn't even vocalize the situation with their father. She couldn't blame him.

A breeze struck the two of them. Billy's recently tended to bowl cut was too short for an effect, but Suzanne's blonde locks blew behind her. She rubbed his head and said, "Nobody is going to tell you a lot of stuff in life is easy. But, it's worth it. Sometimes feeling a breeze is enough to make you forget the worst of what's happened. Even if it's just for a moment."

"Okay." He said flatly as he looked down to the deck, shimmering now from the clear sky.

With a calming smile, Suzanne used her index finger to pull his chin up so he was matching her eyesight. "This guy's an executor of an estate. Mom's estate. It's all complex…"

And boring. Even for me.

"...and not something you have to worry about yet. Maybe even ever, hopefully. This'll be the first and last one of these we go to for a long, long time. Understand? Too bad for you, guess you're stuck with me."

She blew a raspberry as she rubbed her right knuckles on his forehead, eliciting a giggle she found comforting. She loved his smile, and since their father left and mother passed it was a discomfortingly seldom occurrence.

—

The ferry slowed to a stop as it reached the dock. Small waves rippled beneath, splashing against the decaying, wooden supports. Suzanne grabbed her brother's shoulder again and pulled him back towards her as the rush of people, standing all about from the bow to the stern, rushed in. She folded her arms around his chest and held him up to her stomach as people bumped and scurried by. The siblings watched a few jumble up on the thin portside deck. Angry and grumbling, they managed to wedge one person after the next ruthlessly in the main cabin.

"What do they think is going to happen?" Suzanne asked no one in particular.

"What?" Billy replied.

Men and women alike tried to squeeze through on the narrow passage ways lining the port and starboard sides.

A woman was unceremoniously pushed to the side, her stomach pressing against the rail. For a moment it appeared as if she might vomit.

"They all rush in there at once, trample each other. They think that will get their bags in their hands faster?" Suzanne explained while simultaneously asking rhetorically. Still asking no one in particular. The ether. It was an affectation that had gotten her in trouble in school during test time back in the day.

Billy pushed away from her and again leaned on the bulkhead railing, looking down to the shoreline. Barnacles grasped onto the peer, occasionally being subjected to the turbulent, encroaching waves of the arriving vessel. Crabs scurried on the sand, running over the pebbles and breaching the water line, hustling up the shore.

"Looksee, Suzie," Billy began as he pointed to the shoreline, "crabs."

She approached the bow and looked over as well. "Yeah, quite a few. Those aren't the ones we'll have for lunch though. Unless..." She picked him up and held him over the railing. He gave a soft squeal and squirmed his thrashing, little legs.

"Stop! Stop!" He belted through a giggle.

"Ugh, fine, okay, I'll get you a restaurant crab." She joked and smiled.

The crowd had mostly formed itself into a line. Not a firm line, but superior to the cluster the crowd initiated. The siblings' athletic shoes slipped and squeaked on the metallic surface of the ferry's deck as they approached the small door leading into the common area. Above the door read a wooden sign with red glossed text: 'Saloon'.

"Huh, Billy, I guess I was wrong about it being called a cabin."

"It's a saloon?" Billy looked to her, "like from the old west?"

"Uh, well, I guess. Maybe the cabin is to the saloon what the hotel room is to the lobby."

The saloon consisted of four benches, one at the starboard side, one at the portside, and two back-to-back in the center. All were empty now. Their occupants were inching towards the closet with bag upon bag, suitcase upon suitcase, stacked one on top of the other. As an elderly woman stuck her hand between two bags, pushing towards her own, the rectangular bag atop her hand began to fall towards her. As if it were sliding down to smack her square in the chin. In the nick of time, Suzanne caught it, smiled and pushed it back. The woman smiled and nodded, apparently appreciative of the small courtesy not provided by the remainder.

"Thanks, Ma'am," said a voice from behind Suzanne.

She spun to see the sweating saloon server. He wiped the sweat from his brow and flapped his hand, sending the beads to the floor. He had a nametag that read ETHAN.

"It's a madhouse." Suzanne said.

"Always, ma'am."

"Oh, I know. Used to come here a lot as a kid," Suzanne said as she worked her way towards the strap of her suitcase, "this ferry…", her hand grasped her small suitcase's top strap, "might as well be in New York."

She didn't know why she even brought this thing. It was a travel bag that would accommodate a three-night trip. Small, easily portable and, Suzanne hoped, unnecessary. She had no intention of spending one night here, much less three.

"Don't I know it," he said with a sheepish smile.

"Just you and the captain?" A flash of recognition struck her as she spoke. Suzanne could hardly believe it, but this was the same man who had always been here. He must have been working on this ferry for over twenty years.

"For now, miss. Pretty soon, I'll be gone." His tone was eerie, sad.

"Huh?"

"They're gettin' rid of me. People want a soda they'll just put the money in the basket and go on their merry way. They're puttin' cameras right up thar'." He said as he pointed to the roof of the saloon. "Doin' way with me."

"Oh, I'm sorry."

"You the lil' Reynolds girl?"

This startled Suzanne. From the look on Billy's face, he too found surprise in the sudden familiarity.

"Uh…well, yes. Suzanne, and this is my brother, Bill."

"Billy," Billy said as he stuck his hand out. The elderly attendant shook it.

As the attendant politely smiled to her brother, she thought of how this man could be their grandfather. She doubted it, highly, but to the best of her memory she had never met her grandfather on her mother's side.

"Well, you two. We're glad to have you back. Get some old blood pumping through this island once again."

"We're just here to tend to our mother's will, then we'll—" Suzanne started before the attendant cut her off as he leaned against his tiny bar work station.

"Wonderful woman, that mother of yours. Wonderful."

"Yes," Suzanne said through what she hoped was a polite enough smile. Still, she was through with this conversation. "Well, we're gonna be on the way. Okay, Billy?"

C'mon kid, save me. She thought.

"You two should stay. Beautiful island. Beautiful people. We'd, well, we'd love to have you."

After a beat, Suzanne smiled and walked past the attendant, grabbing Billy's hand.

As the siblings disembarked the vessel, Suzanne *thwipped* and clicked her wear-over shades onto her glasses. Somehow, she had forgotten their existence throughout the ninety- minute duration of their ferry trip. Her mind was occupied, too occupied for sunglasses, at least. They clicked and nearly locked, though two of the four metal curves hung ajar. She fixed them with one final click as she moved the right side up just a tad, it's groove fitting firmly atop the thin steel frame.

"Alright, you ready?" She asked her brother.

191

Billy began to run forward. "Yes!" He yelled, excited.

"Wait, wait. Don't run off. There are only, like, two hundred people on this island but I still don't want you to get lost. We won't be here long. I hope." Towards the end she was speaking more to herself.

The ferry both arrived at Matchstick Island and departed Matchstick Island exactly two times each week. It would arrive and allow tourists several hours, then depart. This occurred on Saturdays and Wednesdays. Suzanne had little intention of waiting four days and some change to depart. This trip needed to be...expedited in its duration.

"Can't we stay here overnight?" He asked as he turned back to face her on the pier.

"Absolutely not. It is both expensive and boring." A local gave her a snide look. She moved up towards Billy and lowered her voice. "I want neither. Watch your step, don't walk backw—" she started as Billy's right heel caught a missing segment in the peer. He fell backwards. His lower back echoed a thud as it slammed to the wood. He looked down to see little white bumps growing between the panels. One such bump, he could see now it was a mushroom cap, was smashed to near dust, some particles clinging to his shoe.

Suzanne had gotten used to his crying, and expected it now. She was surprised, in a positive way, to see him lift himself back up and approach her. "I'm okay," he said.

Before she could even process rushing to his side, a gull wavered into her peripheral.

Its tiny talons fumbled around her skull, scraping her glasses. The talon scraped down her cheek, its body flapping wildly around her head. As it departed, its thin leg kicked upwards, knocking her glasses, and the heavy sunglass shield, onto the pier. It clacked and held upright, straight. As she bent down to retrieve them a gust blew in, common to the island, and sent them tumbling in between two of the pier's planks. Even with the water current bashing into the rocks lining the shore, she could hear the plopping sound of them hitting the water. The gull hovered down to the shoreline and grabbed a very small crab and flew off with it. Suzanne stared, her vision hazy and temper elevating, until it was out of her sight.

With a huff, she rubbed her palm against her head violently. Almost enough to give herself a friction burn. She looked to her brother, rose, and walked over to him. He was just staring at her.

"I'm okay," he said.

She bent over and brushed his jeans. Old Navy, where all his clothes came from. The dust and nearly microscopic wood shavings from the pier transferred to her hand. With a few brushes of one on the other, her hands got as clean as they could with the hand-to-hand sweeping. Then, a pinch struck her nerves. Nothing major, nothing debilitating. Just annoying. A splinter.

Oh, awesome, she thought.

She pulled it from her palm and flicked, reaching down for her brother's hand.

They held hands as they made their way past the pier towards an open-faced restaurant with a front bar and two employees each running around, preparing the orders for the cavalcade of tourists who didn't know to avoid this low rent joint for the far superior two seafood restaurants on the island.

"Can we eat?" Billy asked.

"Not here. Nothing here that isn't at a McDonald's. Further into the island there's a better place. Owned by our family, actually." She responded in a manner colder than she appreciated in immediate hindsight.

She decided it best to engage in some flippancy, the way many do when they fear they've been curt.

"Roger Wilco?" She asked with a smile. "That's what you say on the Xbox, right? On those games I probably shouldn't be letting you play?"

"Just Roger. Or Wilco. I guess not both. What's the word when two things mean the same thing?" He asked.

"Repetitive? Or maybe synonymous."

"Yeah, repetitive." He barely got out the word, pronouncing it as *repe-ti-titave*.

Larger words could serve as stumbling blocks for her brother. At least, now, he was trying. There was a time, shortly after their father's disappearance that his heart would be far from 'in it'. With practice, though, they harnessed strategies to deal with his stuttering. Since the beginning of the ferry trip, though, he had seldom stuttered. Nerves tended to bring it out most in him. Yet, even with all the stress that was orbiting his life, there was nothing now. She figured he felt the way she did. And if that were the case, he'd be stuttering up a storm.

Kid isn't nervous, but I am. That's a first, she thought

as they began to make their way to the center of the island.

Lingering with them was the wafting odor of the cheap and

frozen hamburgers.

II – No One Likes Meetings

The two siblings strolled down a narrow street. It was more of a pathway, just big enough for two golf carts—the only transportation source allowed on the island save for one's own two feet—yet it was still the widest street on the island. It was made of loose cobblestone. No pavement trucks had made their way down this narrow corridor of a road in quite some time, and it would stand to reason that it would be time still before a reappearance. The island's infrastructure could be compassionately referred to as 'rustic'. Most of the residences were more akin to trailers and, save for the island's two hotels, two main restaurants, and the church, all structures were ranchers.

They saw one trailer with cheap, fading blue paint. On its porch, at least a patio reminiscent of a porch, there were bird feeders, all empty. Perhaps more decorative. They, too, had seen better days. Looking at the feeders, Suzanne took the moment to notice a substantial number of gulls flying above them. They'd swoop over them, not close enough to be noticeable or jarring, and hover with the siblings' movements. Then they'd move on, circle around, and hover above them again. Looking back over to the yard, scanning it, she noticed something else unusual. All over the yard were mushroom caps, purple and rotted, most leaning towards the earth as if on their last legs.

Suzanne didn't remember the presence of mushrooms, nor did she remember all of the structures being in such a state of decay. Dried slabs of paint peeled from the trailers and small houses in thick droves. Had she been paying more attention to the path in front of her as opposed to her surroundings she would have seen the bicyclist up ahead.

Its little bell startled her out of her waking dream. As did the bicyclist's decision to ride directly in between the siblings, breaking their hands apart.

"Hey!" The bicyclist, a young man with no helmet— about sixteen, Suzanne figured— yelled.

"S-sorry!" Yelled back Billy. He waved his left hand to his side swiftly several times. Suzanne noticed a red mark already forming.

"Why don'tcha get back thar on the boat. Get back to where ya come from?!" The bicyclist belted out.

With both of her hands free, Suzanne held them out to her sides as if argumentative. "I am where I came from ya little snot!"

"Oh yah?!" The bicyclist ground to a halt, approaching a perpendicular street, both paths circumnavigating a massive church, by far the biggest structure on the island save for the water tower. "Well...we got enough problems with the island now. Nothin' you can do! Just stay out of the way!" He turned back, looked up to the church and began peddling his way out of Suzanne and Billy's sight.

Nothing we can do? Suzanne thought. *That was weird.*

She was aware of the consistent sea level rise prior to coming to the island. It was moderately publicized on local news, not nearly a large enough epidemic to be covered nationally. The fact that it was covered at all was mostly due to a purveying in-state worry about sea level rise. The island had certainly fallen victim to this worrisome trend over the past one hundred and fifty years. About two thirds of its landmass was now consumed with salty bay water, never to be stepped upon again. Whether or not the residents of the town were willing to admit the apparent impending lack of habitability to themselves was…questionable. Still, this must have been what the bicyclist was referring to when he said 'we've got enough problems on the island'.

It was certainly apparent to her, though, even as she had walked down the pier. Whereas once half of it was positioned over land, now it stood over water until the very end. Her times here as a child, prior to Billy's birth, were a little sketchy memory-wise, but she remembered that. Odd.

She grabbed Billy's hand and they continued down the cobblestone street.

"That was nice of you," Suzanne said, "to apologize to that kid. But, look Bill, you do that a lot. You know that? You don't have to apologize for things that aren't your fault."

"I know. But...but I just want people to like me. Apologizing makes them like me, because we don't fight."

"Kiddo, not fighting and being friends are two different things. One's being, I dunno, passive, and the other is building a connection. I can't be your best friend forever, as much as I'd like to be. Wouldn't be healthy for ya. Look, Halloween's coming up. What do you want to go as? We can pick a costume that would go with other costumes and you and a few friends can tag team. Like, I don't know, go as a few characters from a video game you all like."

Billy wiped away a tear as he said, "all the kids say I'm going to go as an orphan for Halloween."

This made her mouth hang open. *Jesus Christ*, she thought. The blind cruelty of children was nothing new, but that kind...unacceptable.

Moisture swelled in her eyes. She hoped it was just the sopping moisture in the air, but it was more. She wanted to be by his side every day yet knew she couldn't, not at all moments at least.

Then, she snapped out of it. A bird fell from its hovering and landed right in front of them on the cobblestone with a smack. It twitched, twitched some more, gave a weak squawk, and passed on.

The siblings stopped cold. Suzanne held Billy back with her right arm. She stepped over the carcass and watched Billy do the same, his eyes never leaving the gull as he did so. Seeing his face, empathic and horrified, she felt even more tears welling up. Even with the moisture obscuring her vision, she could see an unfamiliar structure just up ahead to the right. *Keep it together, almost there.*

They reached the front of the structure.

How odd, she thought as she stood before Buckley Firm: a small, one-story little rancher that served as the town's little law firm. Despite her vast familiarity with the island, there had never been a reason for her to know this particular building until now. It had been here, though, when she was a child. She remembered that for sure. It just wasn't one she ever entered. It was cute, though its size made her question its viability.

The up-close sight of the place nearly confirmed as much. Its wooden door was lined with cracks, some wide enough one could practically see the door's interior, like splitting a log and counting the rings. Suzanne pushed the door. A budge, but no real movement.

Billy saw his sister straining, partly because of a supposed obstruction behind the door and, upon seeing her wave her right hand and switch to the left, he knew it was partly because of the splinter as well.

Weeeeee, the door screeched until it slapped against a floor board. The structure was beginning to lean, pushing the boards up ever so slightly on an uneven keel. The obstruction keeping the door from swinging open was the construct itself, misshapen and aged.

The foyer was simple, a few waiting room chairs, an antique store chandelier if there ever was one, and a small reception desk.

"Well, now," a voice croaked out from behind the reception desk. An older man with flaky, white hair poked his head out. He had been leaning to the floor. "Y'*a*ll must be da Reynolds." He pronounced it more like RAY-Nolds.

"Yessir. That'd be us." Suzanne replied as jovially as she could.

"Y'*a*ll get any'ting to eat yet out there?" He asked, his *th* sounds coming out odd. 'There' sounded more like 'tar'.

Suzanne was acquainted with the eccentric dialect of the island's inhabitants. While she had become used to the stressed vowels, she had not heard them in quite some time. It took her a minute to adjust to the point of comprehension.

"Mmm, no, sir. We came right here. Didn't want to waste any of your time," she said.

Or my own, she thought. Business 101, in any meeting when someone says "I don't want to waste your time", it's the poor man's version of "screw off now, please and thank you".

"Eh, well, y'all make sure you get 'round to it 'fore you leave," the man said before waving them into his back office, the sole other room save for the lobby and a tiny restroom to their right. Its size was comparable to that of a port o potty, perhaps even less.

Suzanne nodded before stepping forward, following the executor of her mother's estate. She looked over to Billy and snapped her right index finger from him to two of the lobby chairs. In between them, a sole fishbowl, sitting on a small foyer table positioned against the back wall. This was the extent of the waiting room's entertainment factor.

"Open or closed?" Suzanne asked, gripping the knob of the office door. Little specs of paint were chipping away with age, but no cracks like the front door.

The executor peered up, eyes hovering above the rims of his glasses. His head tilted to the right, eyes matching the now-sitting Billy.

"I'll close it." Suzanne said. The executor nodded and Suzanne did so.

The executor nodded again as Suzanne sat, as if to say "yes, that chair". His mouth opened, pensive, before finally speaking. "Y'all should stop by your family's restaurant after this. Then rent some bikes, work off the crab

cakes." His subsequent laugh was more like a choking bark,

halting and abrupt. In the moment, Suzanne took note of

how this man—and most of the island's residents for that

matter—had a fairly consistent pep in his speech patterns. It

was as if tiny fractions of each sentence were shortened or

excised solely for the sake of expedition.

"We intend to have some crab cakes. Yes, sir."

"Aw, well, dat's good. Okay, diving in, as I am sure

you are well aware, I am the executor of not just your

mother's estate, but also for the entire family, as well. Now,

despite your lack of involvement with the community, you

are entitled to a certain birthright."

A birthright it sure sounds like you want, Suzanne

thought as she plastered on a polite smile. It was nearly

imperceptible, but Suzanne could swear that she detected a hint of jealousy hidden within the executor's tone.

He continued, "I am right dat you grew up 'round here, right?"

Suzanne nodded and smiled politely again.

"Can't believe you'd leave." The executor's tone soured ever so slightly. "Beautiful place, you musta' been crazy to leave this peacefulness."

Here we go, Suzanne thought. She had been getting the feeling that, while the residents of the island were rude to every outsider, they were being outright hostile with her. The looks from passersby alone…

The executor paused and looked to his desk before he looked back to the growingly disinterested Suzanne. "Dis island, it truly is divided between two families.

There's—", he pronounced it more like *tear*, "da odd in and out resident, sure, but mostly tis' island consists of residents holding blood to only one of two families. Even still, we have dat Mayberry feeling. Da people who live here genuinely care about one anoter'. Da court of public opinion is quite popular around here. Tink' about that, at best i—"

"Sir, please," Suzanne held up a hand. "I'm going to have to stop you right there, and I apologize. I actually do not want to hear about it. Not because it's upsetting, but because I actually don't care. I know how this place op—" Suzanne finished curtly as a boat horn emitted from out on the shore. It startled her. There shouldn't have been a horn at this time.

"Is that us? Oh, sh—" Suzanne started before being interrupted by a *shh* from the now-frowning executor.

It wasn't just the executor that stopped her. While the motion was slight, she felt her chair rumble, perhaps even slide.

With his hand thrown onto the desk with a thudding smack, he barked, "Language! Language, in here, Ms. Reynolds." His face eased into a smile as he leaned back into his chair. He hung his hands just on top of his belly, twiddling his thumbs around one another and steepling his fingers.

Suzanne looked blankly, but with a firm and unwavering disposition, directly at the executor. This island really must be different, if a simple little expletive is enough to freak someone out *that* much. Still, she refrained from apologizing. It didn't feel warranted. Her mind focused more so on the fact that, if only for a brief few seconds, the desk and perhaps the room itself had shaken violently. His palm couldn't have caused all that, no way.

His smile, plastered still across his face in a way that made Suzanne uncomfortable, faded as he began speaking.

"Sorry, Ms. Reynolds. See, here, things operate at a fairly different, uh, pace than what I'm sure you're used to. There are guidelines. Guidelines that must be adhered to rigidly. So, first off—"

"First off," Suzanne cut his sentence off short, "we need to get our stuff and get off of this island. I hate it here. My mother hated it here." This elicited a raised brow from the executor and what appeared to be the permanent end to his fake smile. "And, she was right to hate it. You people rely on tourism yet I see them treated poorly. Or, really, us two for that matter. Billy and I."

"Your mother hated this place. That's what you said?" He seemed able to pronounce the *th* in "mother" just fine.

"That's what I said."

Clear frustration rested on the executor's face, yet also a hint of understanding to boot. "Tat's what makes this complicated," the executor began with his trademark hurried form of speaking, "de island itself is what pertains to dis will. There is a stipulation dat you, and your brudder as well, stay here on the island. Furthermore—" he paused as he flipped a page and darted his eyes up to Suzanne, "your father may *not* reside here on the island. Under any circumstances. There's a lot in this document that I...I guess your mother never informed you of."

Suzanne felt taken aback. Still, though, the information did not come as a shock to her. The executor's eyes scanned down to her hand, now gripping the arm of her guest chair. "Well, guess there was something you weren't informed of. We don't speak, our father and us. His kids and spending time with them aren't exactly high up on his to-do list no matter where we live."

The executor placed his hands on his stomach again as he leaned back in his chair. It emitted a squeak that rang through the narrow office, unnerving Suzanne.

Suzanne released her increased clutch on the chair's arm. "Not much point in that. He's crazy. Lives up in Alaska. Nothing to do up there *but* go crazy. And drink. But he had sure done enough of that even without the location change."

The executor nodded, gave a slight smile and looked back down to his paper.

"Oh, right, right. Your mother had mentioned his...absence." The executor, still smiling, flipped through his papers as he leaned back towards his desk.

Then why ask? What are you getting at? She thought.

"But we are not staying here." Suzanne said.

The executor darted his attention back to her. "Pardon?"

"We're not staying here. Even if I'm looking at the...proposition, objectively, it just wouldn't work. I'm in real estate. I can't exactly see anyone here wanting to unload their property."

The executor stared, blank and silent. "So, you're an agent?"

"Broker." She said. "I was a captive agent. Wasn't for me. Switched sides, basically."

She stared at the executor.

"Furthermore," she continued, "he's not being raised here in The Twilight Zone. Hard enough, out there alone…" she looked off through the window, to the sea, only momentarily second guessing her tone.

"Miss, if you would please just let me finish, you may have those concerns…", he started as her gaze remained out the window, "alleviated. Miss?"

With her chin resting in her palm, fingers over perched over her mouth, Suzanne nodded as she gingerly returned eye contact.

"Okay, now, here you would be taken care of. Residency would be provided; a scholarship would be collected for your brother—"

"By whom?" Suzanne interrupted. She held a squinting, confused look.

"Miss?" he replied.

"Who would be paying for this 'scholarship'?" Suzanne replied.

"The community," he said.

"The community." She repeated flatly, with no small amount of disbelief.

"We take care of one another around here. If da boy were to stay, complete primary school here…"

Primary school? She thought and stifled a chuckle.

The executor continued, "He would be able to attend the undergraduate program of his choice."

Suzanne took a pause before responding, "Okay, well, may I see the will for my own eyes? Because—not for one second—do I believe that what you just said is written on that legally binding document."

"I need to read it from start to—"

"We're finished." She said firmly as she rose from the chair. Its back two legs scraped against the wood paneled floor as it slid backwards. The back of the chair bumped the wall just enough to send a reverberation. It was enough to shake free a hastily assembled, hung framed picture of a lighthouse. The lighthouse of Matchstick Island. It shattered on the ground just as the lighthouse did years ago.

"Shit!" Suzanne yelled.

"Miss!" The executor matched her tone and pitch enough to startle her and—it seemed to her—himself. He straightened his posture and pulled his suit. A thin layer of dust puffed from the fabric. For the first time she noticed that there were a few holes in his blazer. All at once, the three remaining pictures on the wall broke free from their haphazard restraints, shattering against the ground in unison. This shocked Suzanne enough to jolt her whole body. Her heels popped up from the ground faster than the time she found a garden snake in her kitchen sink.

—

On top of the front door to the executor's office sat a bell. Billy sat, his right palm cupping his chin, staring at a blank fifth-grade-level math homework sheet.

The bell shimmered with a ring, another, another, then half of one.

Billy's eyes rolled up to see a stranger with his hand grasping the bell. He let go of it and held his hand out as he backed up a bit, as if unsure whether or not it would ring again. His eyes moved over to Billy as he then turned his head.

"Hey, kid." Said the stranger with a smile and a wink.

"Hi." Billy said and looked back down to his paper.

"Sir. You're supposed to say sir." The smile went away just as fast as the wink.

223

Billy looked back up; gaze fixed on the stranger. He was familiar with obtuse strangers, but at least usually he was close to home. Here, he felt out of his element. It was a different world. Quiet, restrained and, up until now, no one had spoken to him, not really at least. He didn't consider this a good conversational start. He only nodded, politely, but in no rush to call a stranger sir. This stranger was intimidating, and he wanted his mom now more than ever. Billy's eyes rolled over to the fish bowl. The fish stared at him.

Just look at you. I'll just look at you. Please, guy, don't talk, don't talk, don't talk to me.

The man sat in one of the two padded chairs across from Billy. He rifled through some papers before looking up again as he said, "Tings not going so well?"

"The homework?" Billy asked as he forced his gaze away from the fishing, staring back, to the stranger.

"Yeah," the man said.

"It's a long story."

"And judging by your progress a failing grade," the stranger said with a cold undertone in his voice.

Were Billy a little older he would have found the word 'judging' to be a curious choice for this man. While his young mind scoured its own recesses for a proper reply, he stared blankly.

"No sweat. Me too, kid." The man said as he *thwipped* the stack of papers over to the unoccupied seat.

More times than Billy could count, his sister had described him as 'timid'. It was a word he had to look up. While he didn't fully agree with her diagnosis, he did understand it. What he liked about being a 'timid' person is, when he was serious, people tended to notice. He hoped the look in his eyes toward the stranger conveyed that.

"You been to any restaurants here yet?" The man asked in a way that made the word sound like "res-tuh-rents".

What? Billy thought. *This guy talks funny.*

The stranger continued, "you get anyting to eat, yet?"

"Uh, n- n- no. No sir." Billy said.

"Dey got dem a little café by the dock down *thar*. Pretty tasty I might say. Pizza. Lots of pizza. You can get anthing you want for toppins'. Pepproni, mushrooms, daggon' fish n' crab as toppins'. But mushrooms, tey've always been my favorite. You stutter a lot boy? My boy—

Mikey's his name, I'm sure you'll get to meet him once you move here—he used to stutter quite a bit. Just the devil's way of holding you back. You just gotta fling him on outta ya."

Billy did not reply.

—

Come on, Suzie, ya gotta do this. Sit down.

Suzanne gave an apologetic smile and sat back down in her chair. She looked down to the pictures that had fallen from the wall. Their gaudy faux gold frames were slightly cracked, and the glass covering the pictures was shattered on them all.

The executor waved as if to dissuade her from having guilt.

As she sat down, she kept her eyes focused just on the window to her right. Not through it. On it. Or, rather, just at the base where a small plant sat in a miniature potted plant. Like her brother, she refrained from eye contact when in tense situations. It didn't help that she felt lightheaded.

The executor scribbled on documents as she asked, "Mushrooms?"

The executor flashed his eyes up. "Pardon, ma'am?" He asked, clearly confused.

She pointed over. "In there. The potted plant. Those are mushrooms, no?"

"White Button, yes." He said and resumed writing. "Why?"

"Dunno, just curious. I've seen them all over the island. I didn't really think of it until now. They're good for you, I know that. Vitamin A, I think," Suzanne said. In the midst of her deflective rambling, a tendency she was aware of yet felt she couldn't quite control, she did find it strange just how many she had seen. Just throughout the five-minute walk from the boat to the executor's office, she figured she had seen hundreds, maybe even thousands strewn by the side of the roads. But, while he was right in them being White Button, they also looked so odd. She thought about this even more as she focused her attention up from the plant, down to the graveyard that sat next to the executor's office. In between each stone sat tons of white mushroom caps. No two looked exactly alike. Their sizes varied, which she didn't find unusual. What she did find unusual was the fact that not only were they sprouted from the ground, they also found themselves attached to the stones themselves. As far as she figured, she was either seeing things or they were part of a mossy covering.

"Vitamin B, actually. Are you looking to the graveyard?" The executor asked.

"Hmm?" She replied at a volume slightly higher than a mumble.

"It's one of two on the island. That one belongs to your forebears."

Suzanne couldn't find the energy to care. Furthermore, her lack of interest was clearly apparent to the executor, who looked on expecting a response.

He continued amidst the deafening silence, "They are known as 'gilled' mushrooms. Residents believe that once one exits their life here on the island, they enter the middle ground. Da dirt, encompassed by water, made whole by the water, is the middle ground."

"So, what, people eat enough of them and they grow gills? That's the theorem at play? You believe that?" Suzanne asked with a heavy dose of trepidation.

The executor grew stern and said, "there are many things in this world dat cannot be fully explained."

She felt her tone had properly conveyed a joke. This did not seem to be the case, at least as far as the executor had read it. She huffed before saying, "apparently not rationally, at least. Believe whatever you want but know *that's* ridiculous." She then flapped her arms over one another and held them close to her sternum. To her right, the window slowly slid up about six inches. A breeze rolled in directly on Suzanne, with her arms already crossed. She didn't particularly notice. After a beat she said, "I'm guessing you eat enough of 'em and you beat Darwin to the punch?"

"Oh goodness no, we don't eat dem on this island. Nor do we believe in the words or ideas of Charles Darwin." The executor said with what Suzanne perceived as growing irritation. He too, now, held folded arms to sternum. His posture had been relatively and subtly rigid ever since she entered the office; perhaps just a professional posture. She knew that posture says more than words sometimes, but she had noticed a hint of relaxation within his professional posture. It ceased to be.

"Life's little ironies."

The executor's eyebrow raised. "Such as?"

"You have the Earth's foremost natural decomposer in a plot of dirt that ostensibly celebrates life. Just humorous, is all. Like my mother dying in our goddamn living room," Suzanne said as she crossed her right leg over her left, inadvertently bumping the executor's desk while doing so. She looked to the executor's coffee mug, which now housed a sliver of a crack streaked down the side.

Did I just do that? I didn't even hit the table hard enough for it to…no, no that definitely wasn't there a second ago. Alright, Suzanne, straighten up. This is almost over. This stupid, stupid shit.

The crack on the mug grew ever so slightly.

Okay, that just happened. Now I really want to leave.

The executor kept his gaze razor focused on her; eyebrows now furrowed. "For your mother, a wonderful woman—"

He paused as Suzanne's own brows furrowed in response.

"Empathy, or at least sympathy. These are qualities befitting the superior person." The executor finished. Holier than thou.

"So, what's going on here? Are we getting our inheritance? Can we just get that—now—and move on?" She asked, then mumbled, "then leave this hellhole?"

He noticed and looked above his glasses at her. Not exactly menacing, but more than perturbed.

"Well, in short, Ms. Reynolds, that proposal is...", he began.

Don't say untenable, don't say untenable

"Untenable." He finished her thought as stern as could be.

Damnit!

There was a slight rapping at the door. Suzanne and the executor both looked to it, but it didn't seem to be someone knocking. Not quite loud enough. Muffled, almost.

"Okay, then, would you like to give me a hint at what you're driving at? You've gotta give me something here. Thus far, this conversation is like cave diving without a flashlight." She raised one eyebrow.

"I'm putting your mother into a…proper perspective, for you," The executor finally said after a delay that she felt trudged into 'awkward' territory.

235

"Yeah, you can keep barking, but I'm the wrong tree." With that, Suzanne harshly slid her chair back, knocking it to the wall. She threw her hands up to her sides in defeat and approached the office door. "My mother was a vain, egotistical, petty shrew of a woman who ran my father off. Don't even ask me if I blame him. Half her vocabulary was loaded questions and the other half was shit talking about people who deserved absolutely none of it. The only thing that makes any sense to me now…is why she would take the mushrooms out of her salad.

III – Even the Best-Laid Plans are Pointless

The door to the executor's office swung open violently enough to smack the right arm of Billy's chair. The clang of wood to wood was enough to startle not just Billy and Suzanne, but the stranger in the waiting room as well.

The chair's arm left a circular dent within the wooden door. But, not just one. There were streaking cracks above the height of the chair arm, four in total. One next to the other, each about four inches apart from the next.

The stranger's mouth hung open as Suzanne grabbed her brother's hand and pulled him up. In immediate hindsight, it was probably rougher than necessary, but a hurry is a hurry. Her gaze barely matched the stranger. "Billy, we're leaving. Pronto."

"But—"

"—Nope," Suzanne cut him off, "no buts. We're done. We're leaving."

The executor stumbled out of the office and looked to the stranger before addressing the siblings. "Ms. Reynolds, *please*, we have more to discuss."

"No. No sir we don't. You act as if I've never seen a contract before. I have. Many of them. And in none of them were there any stipulations as genuinely asinine as what you laid out. Live here? No. I wouldn't live here if we were forced to as part of protective custody." Suzanne held her right index finger pointed to the executor.

The stranger remained focused on his documents in hand as he blurted out, "Miss, you should probably listen to him. Here, you'll have control."

Suzanne looked down to the stranger and gripped her brother's hand tighter.

The nerve on this guy.

Her gaze flashed back to her finger, which remained rigid yet wavering as it faced the executor. "Okay, for one, I certainly do not believe that to be true. In fact, I actively disbelieve that to be true. Furthermore, I believe said fallacy was orchestrated to swindle us. Even furthermore, I believe said orchestrator is standing in this room and—spoiler alert—it's you."

While most of Billy's items were in his one-strapped backpack—stacked neatly in an obsessive-compulsive disorder kind of way—there were a few miscellaneous papers and a protractor sitting on the carpeting beneath the chair. Suzanne began to feel bad about pulling him due to her own frustration and bent down along with him to assist. Their eyes met one another and she put forth her best apologetic smile possible. Relief washed over her as he gave an accepting smile in return.

God he's growing up fast. Looks like Da— No. Suzanne. Stop it.

She held the front door open for her brother as he stepped out into the crisp air and flung the backpack over his shoulder. He looked down to the gravel as they began their steady pace up the narrow street. His gaze remained there, staring below.

More than she was comfortable with, Suzanne wanted to rush off the island. As the frigid breeze struck the hairs on her neck, she wondered if she would feel this uncomfortable even if it were a summer day. She figured so. It wasn't the weather that made her feel so cold. She reached her hand out to find Billy's, but came up only with empty air.

"Kiddo?" She asked in a tone that sounded like an old motor. She looked to her right, no Billy. Her left, just a few more slowly moving pedestrians. Then, she looked behind her. In the distance, she saw him. *How'd he get so far away so fast?*

Billy stood just before the gate of the graveyard. His eyes were razor focused on a leafless tree; the only one in the graveyard. In fact, it was one of the very few on the island.

It, too, was littered with mushrooms all up and down each root that protruded from the earth.

The stranger and the executor stood on the porch of his office, staring at the two of them. They adjusted their gaze to Billy as Suzanne darted them a look. "I'm getting him. I'm getting him," she said grumpily, trying to wave off any further doses of a condescending and scolding undertone.

As she walked over, the executor asked, "what would you like me to do with this document 'den, ma'am?"

"Regift it right to the waste basket for all I care. I'm getting my brother," she then switched to addressing her brother, who was opening the gate to enter the graveyard. "Billy, don't go in there. C'mon," she finished addressing him at a volume that was just under a yelled order.

"I really want to finish 'tis, miss," the executor flatly pleaded.

She grabbed Billy's shoulder and led him down the road, peering back only once as she said, "go ask Mick Jagger about getting what you want."

The executor and the stranger flashed one another a glance. The stranger asked, "Think they'll be back?"

"Dunno. But there'll be real trouble if dey don't."

—

The siblings could see the dock from where they stood. But it wasn't time to head there just yet. Their destination sat to the right. Reynolds Inn, their family's combination hotel and restaurant. A beautiful structure made of aged red brick. The only unfortunate part of its décor was its lime green window frames.

Suzanne thought for a moment. They had time for lunch or dessert at the island's favored location but not both.

"We have time for one of two things, kiddo, ice cream over at 'Stacy's' or lunch. What'll it be?"

Billy tapped his finger against his lips thinking. "lunch," he said.

"You sure?"

Billy thought again then nodded rapidly.

"Alrighty."

The two entered the restaurant. It was full of patrons, mostly out of towners. Those who were residents, peered at them with immediacy. It was uncomfortable, and Suzanne felt a chill creep up her neck.

She barely noticed Billy ask, "what will you get?"

"I, uh, I dunno Bill. My taste buds are far from refined, my palette far from expansive, so I'm sure I'll just stick with crab cakes."

He gave her a perplexed look as they waited to be seated.

She broke the silence. "You?"

"Chicken tenders."

"Chicken tenders?!" Suzanne giggled. "The one thing this place is good for is crab cakes, and you're going to get chicken tenders."

"Yeah, they don't have pizza."

Suzanne gave off a chuckle and then a sigh as she started to pick up on the fact that the hostess had seen them—a while ago—but was sure taking her sweet time to come over and assist.

The hostess, a portly woman with a look that could be kindly called "sour", approached them. She had a nametag that read JEAN. "We're all full," she said coldly.

There were three empty tables, one long enough to suit a family and two four-seaters.

"Miss," Suzanne said, "I hate to disagree but there are—"

"—Them two little'ns for tourists. Big'n's for a meetin of residents later on. You're neither."

How on Earth…?

Suzanne's mouth hung open in shock for a beat before she chuckled angrily, almost adversarial. "Terrific. Thanks so much. Funny, I was just thinking it would be great if this day got ruined even more than it already has been. You've made my wish come true, Jeanie."

She grabbed Billy and they swiftly exited the restaurant. The hostess crossed her arms and peered on angrily, waiting until they were out of the door.

What on Earth? Suzanne thought just before the startling slap of the screen door behind her. She adjusted her tone away from the one she had tiredly used with the hostess to a lighter one for her brother. "Well, I guess no crab cakes. Shame, that's their bread and butter. And butter, apparently."

Don't be mean, Suzanne, even if that woman can't hear you. Be an example.

Just then a strange, irksome twinge at the back of her head. She hoped for a swift headache if there were to be a headache at all.

"And n- no chicken ten- tenders," Billy broke her self-beratement.

"Nope."

Billy looked down. He was definitely sad, though she had doubts that it was just about the chicken tenders. Or lack thereof. She bent down and hugged him. "Well, we're together through thick and thin, kid. Can't have the thick and thin without the thick, and this day's been thick."

"L- l- like that t- time you got really mad at me?"

Suzanne didn't even need more specifics. A few years back Billy had tried to suck a newspaper up a vacuum funnel. It didn't go well. It was the end of that fairly new vacuum. It happened at the wrong time, too. Her stress level had reached a boiling point and it had to bubble out somewhere. Ever since she had been forced to adapt to a more maternal role, she promised herself not to yell at Billy, ever, if she could help it. This had been the example of not being able to help it that she needed to—hopefully—never allow it to happen again.

With time, though, the impact of the moment had softened to the point that Suzanne could now chuckle, then laugh while she said, "yep, like that time."

A thought flashed across her mind. Even without her glasses, her vision hadn't been so bad in the executor's office. Ever since then, though, everything was almost shaped like waves. Billy's stutter was back in full force, too. Even more than usual. Her mind went back to her wavy vision, which only made it worse, which in turn made her feel nauseous.

—

As they approached the dock, Billy ground to a halt. She could feel his absence as only a doting sibling can and turned to see him walking towards the dock café. "Hey kiddo, whatcha' doing?"

"Please Suzie, I'm hungry. Please, I'll be q- quick." Billy pleaded.

"Can't you wait, kiddo? The boat ride's seventy-five minutes." She said in her own form of pleading.

"How long?" He asked.

"An hour fifteen. We get back to the shore, a thirty-minute drive, we eat at Papa Niro's. Could use some comfort anyway, nothing better than Niro."

"I'm hungry now," he said.

She huffed, and felt a rumbling in her own stomach as well.

How were they on time? She wondered. She figured the boat would be ready to depart in twenty minutes, tops.

Billy was persistent, and out of nowhere she wondered for a moment if she was enough for him. She knew herself to be occasionally emotionally distant, but now she feared herself an emotional anorexic.

It was just a quick bite to eat for him. No big issue. Why not get him what he wants. *Because it's time to get on the boat and leave this place.*

No, his needs before yours.

But I didn't ask for this.

Her mind leapt around. Then, her mind went to Papa Niro's. She loved their little life. She loved their little apartment. She loved the very fact that they had their own regular pizza joint. It was emblematic of the life, the comfort, that she had cultivated for the two of them.

Of course, I'm enough for him, she got firm with herself.

It *did* seem a tad silly to delay the inevitable. She shoved her hand into her purse and rummaged through. Her fingers passed over her keys, a pepper spray canister and they darted back upon being poked by the long tip of a single disposable flosser.

She rubbed her thumb against the poked index finger and continued her search until she reached her leather wallet. She pulled it from her purse and unbuckled the overlapping metal piece. She pinched and pulled out a neatly folded wad of bills and flipped a few until she reached a twenty-dollar bill. As she pulled it from the bundle, the remainder nearly flew away from the breeze tickling the shoreline.

In what she figured was either quick reflexes to save the flying bills or a rude grasp for the twenty, Billy was quick to snatch it. The crease of the bill slashed the spot where she was poked, essentially leaving a mark akin to a circle with a line drawn through it. "Thanks Suzie," he said as he began hustling to the café bar.

"Hey-o!" Suzanne yelled.

Billy spun again. "Yeah?"

"Well, aren't you going to ask me what *I* want?" She gave off an intentional and self-aware parental inflection.

"What do you want?" He quipped, replicating her tone.

"You should just ask someone without them having to tell…just get me a slice of pizza. Cheese. No toppings. Don't like toppings."

"I know. Okay. No toppings. Wilco!" He yelled back as he made his way to the counter.

To the left of the dockside diner was the town's school, which covered everything from elementary to high school curriculum. The elementary schoolers funneled out of the trailer-esque school as a bell rang above the solitary door of the unit. Not a bell you'd find in your standard public school; it was the same as the bell that hung over the door of the executor's office. All of the children, single file, held a long ribbon. Upon squinting, she saw it was basically a rope with little bows on it that the children held adamantly. Suzanne knew it to be a trick elementary school teachers used to get kids to stay together when moving. The hard part of playground time is actually getting them to *walk* to the playground.

With a severe jolt, the kids all halted in place and stared at her as she was beginning to turn and move up the dock towards the ferry. Yet again, a chill ran up her neck, which was mirrored by a single drop of blood that ran down her finger. Presumably, it came from the sharp plastic flosser, or the paper cut, or both.

With a raised eyebrow, she turned and made her way up to the ferry. An attendant dressed entirely in white with a little black bowtie stood on the dock and grinned at her as he asked, "And how was your time, miss?"

"Like a carnival ride, in that the operator of the Twisty-Go-Round is passed out drunk and you're stuck."

Jarred, the attendant said nothing. Suzanne smirked and ascended the metallic latter to the port.

—

As she entered the saloon of the ferry to load their bags, she looked out of one of the numerous tiny windows to make sure Billy was doing okay.

What can happen, Suze? It's a damn island. Where's he gonna go?

He appeared to be fine. She chuckled to herself as she saw him get up on his tip toes to reach out and grab the two paper plates, each with a greasy slice soaking through. He started making his way back to the boat. Through another one of the numerous lined windows, she could see him rush back to the server, as if he had merely spun in a circle.

Must have forgotten the change. Always does.

She tossed their bags into the cubby and looked back out. She didn't see him now. Not at the stand. Not on the dock.

"Here, Suzie!" He cheerily and loudly called from behind her.

"Jesus, kiddo! Gimme a heart attack." She grabbed her slice of cheese pizza from him. "Where's yours?"

"Huh? Oh, I put it on the table."

"The table?" Suzanne asked as Billy pointed to his right.

The soda and pretzel bar was now unattended. Odd, she hadn't noticed. Instead, there now sat two baskets, one for soda and one for pretzels. To the left of said baskets sat a paper plate housing a half-eaten piece of pizza with pepperonis and...mushrooms. She looked back to her brother, handed him her cheese pizza and said "eat" as she grabbed the mushroom pizza and threw it out of one of the small windows on the starboard side. It plopped in the water and sank.

She watched Billy's mouth drop just before her attention was drawn to the shore. Like a force guiding her gaze. Perhaps it was the changing tides, but it appeared that the shore had *moved*. As if it had ascended just a bit up the length of the dock.

Just my imagination. Just this place.

Billy rushed to the window to watch the pizza sink into the abyss. Suzanne again looked for the pretzel and soda attendant. Nowhere to be seen. She shrugged it off with a smile and gave Billy a hug.

Along with the soda and pretzel baskets, there was also a photo frame standing on the bar. Inside it was not a photo, but a recent obituary for ETHAN BOWIE.

—

An hour into their return trip, the siblings began to feel antsy. There were some pretty threatening clouds revealing themselves in the sky. The closer they got to them, the tighter their grips became on the steel safety bars of the bow's bulkhead.

In an effort to calm her brother, who she knew well enough to certainly know when he was concealing fear, asked "what's your fear, muh dear?"

"Lightning. What if it hits us?"

"It won't. We're not high enough. If it hits any area of the boat, it'll hit…", she trailed off as she began to look for the highest spot. Above the helm extended a large radio communication pole. She pointed to it and said, "that. It'll hit that. High up. A conductor. But, even still…I doubt it."

"Really?"

"Yeah. I've got a silly little thing called hope."

Suzanne was more worried about the turbulence as the boat leapt above waves and landed with thuds upon the water. The light was disappearing at a rate she found uncomfortable, not because of her own fears, but for Billy. Off the port and starboard sides there were more buoys with flashing orange lights on top of them. Now, though, the darkness mostly concealed the buoys themselves and only allowed the orange lights to sparsely illuminate the surrounding waters.

Well, perhaps I'm a little scared too. Looks bad.

As if on cue, the captain's voice rang over a few speakers dispersed throughout the boat. "Ladies and gentlemen, we should be able to sail right on through this. It seems we just missed it during your visit today. We at Matchstick Tours would like to again thank you for your patronage. Hang tight while we sail through, and you may want to return to within the saloon where we have a variety of refreshments."

As if further on cue, Bolts of lightning erupted from between the two perturbing clouds not too far off. A few miles, maybe less. The closer the boat crept towards them, the darker the circumference around the boat. For a reason she couldn't quite comprehend, the temperature seemed to be rising. Billy, too, wiped sweat from his brow. Beads of sweat streamed down the back of their necks. One such bead ran up, across and down a tiny mushroom cap sprouting from the nape of Suzanne's neck.

Backwoods

1—Woods

Irving Steadman was a man with a record. A man emotionally on the run from his actions and, up until three months ago, the law. These were things he knew.

The law has ceased to fret about deserved armed robbery and manslaughter charges since The Reset. This was something he did not know, as for all that intermediate time he had lived in the woods alone. Mostly alone, that is, as with him always was his Black Lab, Guppie.

With a limping gait and a ragged look, Irving walked side by side with Guppie to his secluded and dilapidated shack in the middle of the woods. He was fortunate enough to be left the secluded property, though not for the purposes of law aversion.

He thought about that just as much as he thought about how it was just a matter of time. Ever since the robbery went sideways, the clock started ticking.

Irving thought about the events that played out ad nauseum. He knew it was starting to consume him, his soul, even.

An innocent young woman had to die just so he could feel financially stable. This was the price that was paid.

If he felt guilt for anything, and he did, it was for not being forward thinking. He should have re-checked the ghost guns' cartridges to confirm blanks. You carry live ammo, you risk a higher penalty.

His life had taught him that time heals all wounds. Soon, he would be reunited with his wife, his baby boy, and his daughter, soon to head out of state for college.

To Irving, reuniting with them was his oxygen. Being separated from his family was akin to possessing three phantom limbs. Longing was not something he was used to. Being in charge, that's what he was used to.

But the financial crisis took everything, not just from him, but from a lot of people. Their small town was affected the same as the world's biggest and most beautiful cities. Desperation had become the new standard for a vast amount of the human race. 2020 had been one hell of a year.

There was a pit forming in his stomach. In fact, the sensation of rumbling emptiness was worse than usual. Worse than it had been for the past three weeks, since

Irving's conceptualization of life was permanently altered. He looked to his companion and scratched him behind his flopping, thin ears. Guppie looked to Irving and rubbed his head on his master's forearm. His ear flopped over then slid down Irving's aged but clear tattoo of an anchor.

For not the first time, I dawned on Irving that he was hugging the current extent of his family. His sigh was reactionary, fully inadvertent.

Guppie's attention quickly diverted away from Irving. The dog observed his surroundings, searching for inconsistencies. His senses tugged, something *was* out there, something was askew, and Guppie knew this far better than his master.

"What's wrong, pal?" Irving asked in his standard thick southern drawl.

Usually, Guppie's head would jolt to so he could match Irving's gaze. That didn't happen this time. Guppie's eyes remained fixed. Staring into the woods. Irving's words failed to register with the dog. The leaves of Autumn fell consistently around the two, the trees now nearly bare. Still, Irving saw nothing. Nothing that should have alarmed his dog, at least.

Guppie's head jerked upward, facing one of said bare branches. Four birds had just flutteringly landed their way on top of it. Each bird was of a different type.

Irving's eyes squinted, as he joined his dog in engaging the birds in a staring contest. That's how it was, too. The birds' vision would not budge. They were weary of Guppie and himself, in direct spite of being far out of reach above.

One of the bird's head bent, curiously, as he chirped.

Ninety-nine times out of a hundred, perhaps even more

frequently than that, Guppie would be barking like mad.

Not unlike most, if not all, other dogs, the birds were prime

prey. They would serve as lovely hors d'oeuvres for a feast

that had been long awaited.

Guppie did not care about filling his belly at this

point, though. His eyes could not leave the birds, as if his

body were out of his control. Suddenly fear struck the

animal. He began to whimper and whine. His master

leaned down in an attempt to comfort him.

As Irving looked back up to the birds, all of their

eyes flash pure black. It was like flipping the blinds from

allowing light to disallowing light to enter your home.

"What the h—" Irving said before a congested and quick

flurry of movement.

270

The birds violently flew from the branch in unison. They traveled further and further into the sky, until they were tiny specs on a vast blue canvas. Irving raised an eyebrow, shook it off, and said, "Nothing, I guess. Have we been up too long, bud? Starting to think maybe we've been up too long. Losing my mind."

Guppie ceased to stand in rigid form, and he darted to the shack, only ten yards or so ahead. Guppie laid on the cot that consumed most of the internal space of the shack. Truth be told, that's all that was in there save for a few opened cereal boxes and bottles of water. It was like a cabin from a 1980's horror movie, but smaller. If a shack is the median point between a shed and a cabin, it leaned more shed.

Irving sat on the cot next to his dog and rubbed his hand slowly down his face. He looked to Guppie and shed a tear.

Irving balled his fists, jittery.

"One more thing I busted up. Right, Gup?" Irving sighed and leaned until his back was against the wall. He bumped his forehead against the wall a few times.

"I'm just sorry I brought you out here, bud. Man's best friend...some man's best friend I turned out to be."

He scooched his body to the right, so his feet reached the foot of the bed. He got under the covers and said, "No choices because of my choices."

2—Memories

Tossing and turning, Irving was getting no sleep. He jerked upright, giving up. Gobs of sweat flew to the foot of the cot from the force of his rise.

Guppie looked up, giving an inquisitive whimper.

"Sorry, bud, don't worry about me. I'll be fine." Irving said slowly. He shot a smile to the dog.

Gently, he put his head back on the ratty, yellow pillow.

"It'll all be fine," he said with a frown as he closed his eyes.

With people after him, Irving had lost his tendency to be a heavy sleeper. No one can sleep like a log when they're worried about waking up to a shotgun barrel in their face. But, this, this was different. Like any person Irving was more than susceptible to the power of memories. This time, it was about his dog.

When Irving and his wife, Sara, got Guppie they didn't care to come up with some illustrious, creative name. They just named him "puppy".

When their daughter, Candace, was growing up they never had much in the way of pets. A few dogs came and went but there were consistent behavior problems. One peed on the couch every time eyes weren't on him. One insisted on trying to jump for the window in the living room. He never made it, considering he failed to take into account his miniscule height. It didn't help that Candace was fairly allergic and the medication seemed an unnecessary expenditure.

Once she turned thirteen, though, her brother was born. It was obvious to all that her little brother Paul was fascinated by animals, so, they got a puppy. Fast-forward to a few years later and little Paul was having trouble with his P's. Puppy the puppy became Guppie the puppy and the rest was history. It's just one of those names that stuck.

Guppie moved up the cot and laid his head on Irving's chest. Irving's hand gently rubbed down Guppie's skull, ruffling his ears with his pinky and thumb.

"I guess it's getting pretty close to your birthday, bud. October eleventh, right?"

Guppie stared at him. After a few silent seconds he gave a whimper.

"Well, I *guess* it's October, now."

The two of them had been in the woods running on three months, now, but it felt much longer. Much, much longer.

"I wish I could get you home to see Candace and Paul, Gup. Really wish I could. Hopefully, we'll just be out here a little longer." He pronounced "here" as "har".

For whatever reason it hadn't occurred to Irving that it was outright odd that no one had run across their path. Not in general, of course; he thought about that every day, but not on this day. Their little cottage was in the middle of the woods but it wasn't on Mars. Logistically, over the course of ninety—or however many—days, someone should have stumbled across them. That's not even taking into account the fact that not only had he held up a bank, getting away with a scant $12,000, but a girl had died in that bank. People should be out in droves looking for them. It's not as if no one saw the getaway car. It's not as if it couldn't be identified in the small town, sitting next to the woods behind that decrepit old gas station. Hell, it wasn't even a getaway car. It was a getaway truck.

3—Haywire Job

Stupid shithead Freddie.

You just had to get the date right. The day the Brinks truck comes, collects, and goes. Then, we'd just get in, get out while the money's being transferred to the armored truck. Take advantage of the controlled process and warp it in to expedited chaos. You just have to have the right day.

His own job had been getting the supplies. Masks, dummy guns, fingertip padding, ditch-able getaway ride. Irving had gotten it all. As a CDL-toting truck driver, he usually drove his own rig. You cite it as stolen, insurance moves in. You add a few bruises to your cheekbones, feign that you fell asleep in some parking lot off route whatever-the-hell. "Officer they came out of absolute nowhere! Jumped me! Ripped me right out of the damn cab!" In short, Irving's half of the equation was covered.

To the best of Irving's knowledge, Freddie had catastrophically bungled his sole job. Not to mention, at some point, Freddie swapped out the blanks for live ammo. Or perhaps the weapon itself. No. Why ditch a ghost gun? Untraceable, functional…but they were supposed to be using blanks on this job. Irving had even confirmed it, stressed its importance. Main point being, never take a job unless you're one hundred percent sure of the stature of your…coworker.

—

They met in a diner. A twenty-four-hour diner at an

hour where there wouldn't be, well, diners. The kid,

Freddie, was an enigma to Irving, initially. When Irving

would do a diamond job back in the day, before the advent

of in-depth security systems, he would use a fence. He

should've known not to work with Freddie because the

fence, Jon Kash, claimed he knew next to nothing about the

kid. Just do the job anyway, Kash had said. It'll be quick,

not enough time for too much to blow up anyhow.

Yeah, right.

Look, Kash had said, I've worked with him once

before, he's good. A little abrasive, but that can be reeled in.

At the diner, Freddie arrived late. Two A.M. is just that, two A.M. For decades, Irving's pick-up and delivery schedule had been nightmare after nightmare. And he had made every…last…stop on time.

Freddie got there at 2:11 A.M. No apology, but eyes red as a McIntosh. He flopped himself on the cushion with an abrupt squeak and a *frump* sound as the air escaped from a tear in the upholstery, with feathers sticking out.

Too much attention. Any attention is too much attention. Strike two. If there was anything worse for smooth proceedings than lateness, it would be attention of any kind. Anonymity is the name of the game. It always had been the name of Irving's game.

"What'd he tell you about me?" He asked.

"Seriously?" Asked Freddie with the slightest eyeroll and a heavy grin. He threw his arm over the top of the restaurant booth.

"Yes," Irving, dryly.

With a smirk, "That you're a pain in the ass to work with."

"Sounds about right. So, why'd you volunteer?"

"Because I don't believe everything I hear. And, shit, I need the cash. No need to blow smoke up ya ass."

"Not a great reason. Fine reason, maybe. You need to understand I have a certain way of doing things and not everybody gets rubbed the right way by that."

"Well, me too," Freddie said with a quickness that irked Irving. He lacked humility. It was as if the kid was barely listening; too eager.

"Well," Irving took the moment as the right one to be arch, "for *now* at least, we're doing things my way."

My job. You just happen to be lucky enough to be here. Irving thought this and more as he waited for Freddie to speak.

"That's the thing, Irv, my way *is* your way. I looked you up. I did my research. Your...*controversial* decisions were no different than anything I'd do."

Irv? Irving thought.

"Okay," he said, admittedly a bit flattered. "But, no names. That'll be the first and last time you'll use my name. Certainly not the shortened version. Don't do that again."

"Understood," said the kid as he looked to the table and fumbled with his empty mug. It fell over, shattering. Was the kid nervous? Either way he now had a cut on his finger. It bled and bled until he wrapped it in a bit of table cloth instead of the very reachable napkins. Another strike. Why leave your DNA every which way? Not that it mattered at this very moment but, still, you never know.

In hindsight, Irving knew he should have picked up on a foreboding amount of arrogance, stupidity, and lack of professionalism right then and there. And he did, to an extent. But he also figured this Freddie could be a firecracker and that's not always so bad. You just have to light the fuse at the right time.

"In truth," Freddie said and watched Irving's dwindling attention level spark up, "I haven't been on too many jobs." He pulled the table cloth off of his still bleeding finger. Suffocating the wound had done nothing. He stuck his finger in his mouth before pulling out a pocket knife and slashing a bit of table cloth off. He wrapped it around the oozing wound. "Sorry, sometimes I don't stop bleedin'."

Irving sat still with a disgusted look. Hardly veiled. "Anyway, I want more," continued Freddie. "But I guess you can't strike oil without digging through some dirt first."

—

Yet again, Irving bolted upright on the cot.

"When did he switch out the pistol? And he...he wouldn't go about that alone. He'd have to be..."

Irving looked down to the nodding off Guppie and smiled, embarrassed.

"Talking to myself, yeah? Must look perty strange."

He rubbed the dog's head fervently, ruffling his fur to the point that strands floated down to the wooden planks. Some even slipped through and mixed in with the dirt that constituted the middle ground between each and every plank.

Could he have just been some nut? Kash hardly lets anybody join the party, ever, much less a junkie or whackjob.

"Either way, that boy went in there ready to kill." Irving again vocalized his thought, startling Guppie, who had already begun to go back to sleep.

No, not ready. He wanted to. Sonofabitch had bloodlust.

Irving was right. En route to the bank, Freddie had realized that the provided gun had blanks. He had not been informed of this prior Freddie swapped out his cartridge and tossed the dummy cartridge in a steel sidewalk trashcan. Thankfully for him, it didn't make too much noise. With his mind on the job, Irving perhaps would not have noticed even if it had.

What also was on Irving's mind was the location of the Brinks truck. It should be out here, with one guard to boot. But, all around the two men in front of the bank, there was just that: the two men and no others.

There were questions, and the answers were inside the bank.

Upon entering the bank, the teller told them over and over again that the extraction date was the next day.

Freddie held the gun up to her head. Even through his mask, Freddie's eyes made it clear he was seething. She cried, and as Irving grabbed Freddie's shoulder, he pulled the trigger.

Irving didn't expect anything to happen besides a flash, but he'll never end up forgetting the girl's head just...shattering. Papers lined against the wall were painted red before her chair flew back, her body strewn across the blue carpet.

"What did you do? What did you *do?!*" Irving screamed. It was too late for screaming to do a damn thing.

Irving just stood there, shaking, as Freddie went to the next teller. All Irving could hear was ringing. Not from the shot, but from the shock. His peripheral vision caught Freddie scream at the teller, hand him the bag, wait, then whip the bag over his back. A wicked Saint Nick. But then he flipped it back in front of him.

Irving began wiping his face up to down, as if subconsciously trying to wake himself up to speak. *Dye pack,* he thought.

Freddie opened the bag slowly, aimed right in the direction of the teller. No blue ink. The teller probably didn't want to risk pissing off what was clearly a madman.

Irving wasn't having it either. Something had to be done.

But then Freddie pointed at the teller girl to go in the back. Before she moved, he gave her a smaller variation of the leather sack that was now filled with cash. Irving started lumbering towards the door of the bank. His body swayed like he was finishing a bender. The ringing in his ears from the gunshot persisted.

Then, Freddie was in front of him, waving his hand. The young man snapped his fingers several times. Each time his grimace grew more pronounced. Around Freddie's finger-snapping arm was the smaller leather sack. In his left hand was the larger leather sack, which he pushed on Irving. With his hand free, Freddie pulled his pistol out from his waistline.

Before the foggy Irving knew it, they were outside in front of the bank. He demanded Freddie's weapon which, surprisingly, he handed over. There was hardly a moment before Irving held the gun to Freddie's head.

Irving's eyes scanned the gun as he held it rigid, the barrel mere inches from Freddie's head. This one had serial numbers. The son of the bitch *had* ditched the assigned ghost gun, not just the cartridge. Stupid, rookie move.

"Whattya' gonna do, Irv? Shoot me? Dude, I'm a hemophiliac, you don't even *need* a gun to kill my ass."

"Maybe not, but I have one," Irving said as he pulled the trigger. For the briefest second, he watched Freddie's face go from one of untamed joy and anger to flat shock. The kid really thought Irving didn't have it in him.

Irving snatched the bag off of Freddie's lifeless body, got in their getaway truck, and roared off. In the back seat was a frantic Guppie.

—

Guppie moaned, tossed, and turned on the cot. With hardly anything in their little three-room shack—"the can, the cot, and the kitchen"—Irving couldn't blame the dog for being restless.

"I'm so sorry, Gup. You're stuck out in this microscopic shithole. Nothin' to play with. But it's not about the things you have but the memories you hold, right? Still, I should've dropped you off at the house after—"

A rustling outside. Guppie darted his head up for just a moment. He lunged forward on the cot and placed his paws on the seal of the cabin's sole, tiny window. With razor sharp intensity Guppie wasn't so much peering out at the forest as he was looking through it.

"I heard it too. What is it, bubba?"

Guppie began barking, looked over to Irving, then back out the window to bark some more.

Creeping death was beginning a full-on sprint.

His mind lied in whispers.

You will not be okay.

There's simply too much.

You, my friend, are alone.

Irving reached beneath the cot and grabbed his double-barreled shotgun. He elbowed the rickety door open and aimed the weapon all around. Nothing.

A growling echoed around the bare forest. At first Irving thought it was Guppie.

No, no I can hear him behind me. This is...from out there.

"Now, whoever you are, you just step right on out. This is private property."

Lie.

This makeshift cabin of his was on state-owned land by this point. His uncle's estate had turned it over for the government to fully own as part of a state park. It just happened to be a state park that hadn't been tended to in quite some time. His uncle had just built it twenty-odd years ago when he worked as a ranger. They let him do it, people seldom came out this far.

Anyway, who'm I talking to? It's a damn dog. Well, most dogs have owners. Where are you, beast? Scaring my dog...and where's your master?

"Come on! Out! Out with you, now!"

A white paw lurched out from behind an oak tree

dead ahead. Irving lowered the double-barreled shotgun to

aim it just above the ground.

It was not a dog. It was a wolf. Gray fur with streaks

of white, the wolf moved slowly from behind a thick tree

until he was fully in Irving's eyesight.

"Holy shit." This could very well have been the

biggest wolf Irving had ever seen.

Its mouth was drenched in blood, as were his paws.

Irving looked around with the intent of spotting a dead deer.

No deer, no nothing, just barren oaks and falling leaves. The

wolf raised his paw to his open jaw and began slurping the

blood from between his toes before lowering it. It then

looked dead-straight at Irving.

It was one of those moments between man and nature, man and beast. Their eyes matched and held steady. Then, the wolf's eyes nearly flipped, without so much as a blink, to pure black with a tiny white spec of a pupil. Hardly even there.

Then, in what could only be described as an anomaly of nature, the wolf grinned. Blood dripped from his jagged teeth. From this distance they appeared, well, cracked. Broken.

It lunged towards the shack in a full gallop.

Before Irving could fire off a shell, Guppie burst out of the window and intercepted the charging wolf. A cringey smack ripped across the air as the two animals' bodies met. The two tussled on the ground, blood ripping through the air until the wolf had Guppie by the throat. The left corner of its mouth etched up into a grin again as his black eyes darted up to Irving. They almost beckoned him, as if to say "I'll do it. I'll do it right now. Try me."

Irving bent to his knees, and placed the shotgun on the ground, his finger still wrapped and hovering shakily over the dual triggers.

Only five or so feet away now, the wolf lunged at Irving, who yanked the shotgun from the ground and pulled tight on the triggers. He had grown weak out here over the course of the past two months. Poor diet, exhaustion, insomnia. Still squatting, the kickback of the shotgun blast sent him back.

As he lay back, mud in his eyes and a worrisome sting in his back, he braced himself for the wolf's assault.

But there was nothing. Irving wiped the mud out of his eyes and saw that he had blasted a hole right through the wolf.

It had flown through the air, thudding against the Oak a few feet away. Now it lay motionless on the ground.

"First sign of life in two months and it's a damn rabid wolf," Irving said as he moved to Guppie's side and stroked his head.

Guppie was hurt badly. His eyes were fluttering as if going into shock, and he gurgled blood.

—

In this moment more than any other, Irving desperately wished he hadn't chucked Freddie's gun into the trash can in front of the bank. It went down like this: Prior to getting in his truck to take off as fast as he could from the bank, he ditched Freddie's serial numbered pistol into the trashcan. From this same trashcan he snatched up the ghost gun.

He got what he needed as he memorized the serial number, which he then typed into the Notes app on his phone. Time to get some answers on this kid.

But, first, a tough forty-five-minute drive up Interstate Ninety-Five to the mansion of one Jon Kash.

This hope was dashed as he got about a quarter-mile away from the entrance lane. What he saw just before he moved below a beautiful, classic brick overpass, was a barricade of police vehicles. They weren't all sedans, either. They came prepared, suspiciously prepared. Lined along with the red and blues was what appeared to be a SWAT vehicle, an armored van.

Even if he hadn't heard a sudden amount of noise from the highway above, he would have known that the plan to hoof it to Kash's was done. Intermittently looking up to the road in front of him, Irving texted TREY – AUTO BODY – FAMILY FRIEND the following: *Open garage, Coming 2 U, Happening now.*

He waited for a reply, again darting his attention to the road in front of him. Hardly anyone else on the road. In his rearview mirror, no one. So far, so good. Just as he was about to put his phone down, up popped the three wiggling bubbles indicating an impending reply.

Then it went away.

Disgruntled, Irving growled softly.

The bubbles came back up briefly before they were

replaced with: *Ok. I will be waiting out front.*

Oh boy, he's pissed, thought Irving.

—

Upon arriving at T&M AUTO, Irving saw no one

sitting in front of the shop. No one on the perpendicular

streets surrounding them. And, still, *no* sirens.

The eeriness of the situation put some further pep in Irving's step as he stored the truck in the open garage and just about closed the door.

Before exiting the garage, he darted back into the truck's cab and snagged both the large and small sacks. Remaining in its customary placing in one of the center console's cupholders was his cellphone.

He looked around for another getaway vehicle, yet the only one he saw was a ratty sedan with chipped red paint and two missing wheels.

As he started for the garage door to begin his search for a replacement, or Trey, shop owner and friend of the "Family".

He just hoped not to see Matt, the other co-owner who was *not* a friend of the "Family". Matt put his foot down on business being done on T&M property.

Then, it wasn't so much who he saw as it was what he heard that scared the hell out of him. It was a woman's particularly sharp scream. He turned around frantically yet saw no one.

Unrelated?

No. Can't risk it.

Then he finally heard sirens. What, had they forgotten about him and moved on to whatever was happening here with this woman? Or, were they just so slow that they were just now catching up with him?

Something really *was* off around here. With that thought he felt the desire for comfort wash over him like ice water. As if instinctively, he looked to the rear of the auto

body shop. A thick line of trees. The woods of the public

park and, within it, a temporary home.

As he began his venture out to his uncle's property,

once he knew he was out of sight, he wiggled open the small

sack and peered in. Diamonds. Not part of the plan.

—

The large and small sacks remained in the same

places they always were. The large sack sat beneath the

floorboards of the shack. The small sack sat in the large pocket of Irving's cargo pants.

As much as he regretted not having Freddie's gun, he regretted not having his cellphone even more. Even if turning it on now meant getting caught, it would be worth it to get someone to meet him even halfway out here. At least, then, Guppie would have a fighting chance.

While his threshold for accomplishment was always fairly low, judging by his schooling experience—or, rather, comparative lack thereof—this moment now was one he knew he had to grab by the throat. Weary, he bent to his knees, feeling his right one shift and crack along with his back, thanks to the poorly balanced cot, and picked up Guppie.

"Oh, sweet hell," said Irving as his back cracked yet again upon standing up straight.

It's evening, he thought as he looked towards the setting sun. *West.*

Cradling Guppie, he set off through the same three mile stretch of woods he traversed leaving from the auto body shop.

Above him, a black-eyed bird squawked. Irving did not look up, doggedly persistent in his new journey.

4—More Time for Introspection

What do wolves and birds have in common?

And what could make their eyes switch over like that?

Never before had he seen such a thing and it was, in

a word, unsettling.

He shook his head as if her were wiping clear the

Etch A Sketch board of his mind.

No, no. Shut up. Don't think, just move.

He moved his increasingly sore and exhausted

bones.

He looked down to Guppie, his eyes almost misty and grey, staring back up at him. For the first time since he was a puppy, the dog looked like a swaddled baby.

"You know something's wrong out here, right?" Said a voice from behind him. Irving's startled heart could have stopped were it not for some sort of…familiarity.

He turned to see…himself. Standing there, arms crossed, eyebrow raised. He even had the same anchor tattoo on his right forearm.

"You've been out here for months, and—", the mirror image put his hand over his eyes and pantomimed looking around the forest as if he were surveying a crowd for a friend. "—Nobody. Not a soul. You and that, uh, example of knowledge neglect Freddie *killed* that girl. That's right, you too. You were there, you're just as culpable."

"Get out of my head." Irving begged with a wheeze and a wince.

The mirror image huffed like a horse and said, "Slick, I'm not in your head. I am your head."

"I been out here too long."

"That is true," said the mirror image, "but that alone is not why you're seeing me."

"Please…"

The mirror image's tone sharpened. "Hey, that's what the *girl* at the *bank* said! Good memory! And then you stepped in—realizing the error of your ways—and stopped Freddie from ensuring that day would be her final in a not-so-long series of them."

The mirror image was matching Irving's pace, step by step. His southern twang, too, matched Irving's. "What

309

you did was stand thar like a goon." The mirror image squinted his left eye and waggled his left index finger up and down as he said, "See, you knew it was wrong, and worse yet you knew it was gonna happen. I bet you knew it was going to happen before you even stepped inside the bank."

"No, I— I didn't. I didn't know."

"Mmhmm, so you figured Freddie a well-adjusted fellah from the get-go?"

"No. Well, no, I guess not really."

"'Not really.' Wow. Listen to you. Forty-seven years old and still got a head of bricks. Momma'd say 'So many bricks that, were your head a house, it would be a sturdy one'."

"You're just another hallucination, like the birds' eyes."

"And the wolf's eyes? The wolf itself?"

Irving paused, thinking. "Yes—well, no—not the wolf itself."

"Yeah, hate to break it to ya but it's all real. What you need to know is that I'm your guardian angel…of sorts."

"Like in *It's A Wonderful Life*?" Irving asked with a rhetorical tone.

"If that helps."

"But the guardian angel in *It's A Wonderful Life* wasn't identical."

"That's where you draw the sanity line? That your situation isn't identical to *It's A Wonderful Life*? Unbelievable. Listen, what you also need to know is that the reason no one is out here in a search party looking for your ass is that thar are far greater global fish to fry. You're in a world now where a single homicide...well, it's minor. Get what I'm saying?"

"No."

"Yeah, okay I'm not explaining this well. Look, as bad as you think life is, somethin's happened that is worse than you can imagine."

The mirror image ramped up its pace and walked backwards in front of Irving. In this moment Irving thought of the scant differences between himself and the mirror image. For one, it was sprightly whereas his knees weren't doing him any favors. He also found the mirror image to speak more quickly, louder than himself. Though that wouldn't be hard, he's always chosen to speak low. The last thing was something picked up on by Irving's experienced instincts: the mirror image sure didn't seem like it was about to reveal *every*thing.

"For the past few months, a *ton* of people have been dying, alright? Isn't that starting to make sense to you? If there *were* people in the town, they'd be looking for you, right? You still with me?" The mirror image held his arms out.

"So where are the people?"

"You've heard of ascension, no?"

"Sure, like the Bible. The Rapture."

"Yes, just like the Bible."

"Is that what happened?"

"Sort of, but then why would the black-eyed spooky animals be after you?"

"Are they?"

The mirror image rubbed his right hand up and down the bridge of his nose. "…Yes."

"Well, why Guppie?"

"Because Guppie got in the way."

"And what are you, then? You don't seem to be much of a guardian."

"I used that term to kind of facilitate your understanding. Glad it worked. No, I'm what you should've had a while ago, some common sense. This, Guppie, this situation…it's a test, man. At first accidental,

314

now a test. Free will and destiny intertwining, as they are

wont to do."

"A test for what?"

"Seriously? Jesus, a test to see if you'll do the right

thing."

"Turn myself in?"

"Uh-yuh. Amongst other things." The mirror image

was clearly growing more impatient, contentious. With that

being said, Irving still figured he was slipping under the

blanket of psychosis.

"I will...I can't do this anymore." A tear rolled down

Irving's face.

"I'm hoping so. That's why you've been spared from

the Descension...or 'The Reset', as the news has been

referring to it, for so long. You got potential, slick, it's just taking you a hell of a long time to realize it."

"Like how it's taken me a long time to realize that people aren't actually after me."

"Yes, now you get it. Look, you basically live in Mayberry. You drive a whopping nine miles to rob a bank in the very next town and think that's enough distance for no one to recognize and subsequently be able to find you."

"I was cautious. Gloves, mask, I left that dickhead's gun behind. As far as they know, the cops, it was Freddie and John Doe who robbed that bank. I'm forward thinking."

"You're Andy Griffith with a rap sheet, of course people would be able to find you, even if you dump the truck and run into the woods. You're an idiot, not evil. That's why you've been spared. There will come a time where you'll be able to prove whether or not that is truly the case." The mirror image stopped speaking, allowing Irving to mull it all over.

"I had the best intentions. My daughter, she's what I should have been. If I can't even pay for her *school*…"

"Yeah, intention is a factor. But, so was Freddie."

"A factor…in me being spared?"

"Yup."

"But, why? I killed him, and murder is a mortal sin."

"It is, and while your initial inaction docked you some points, as it were, in the most technical and objective sense killing him in front of the bank was a 'good' thing."

"Okay." Irving stopped in his tracks.

The mirror image sighed. "Because you killing him stopped something even more negative. He would've killed again that day, and as it turns out, another eleven people throughout the next three years. He was only going to last about three years before being splattered by a truck. He essentially would've become a hitchhiking killer. Eventually he goes out on the interstate," the mirror image pantomimed walking with his index and middle finger, "tries to wave down an eighteen-wheeler, the driver of which would have been quite sleepy. Bam. Eleven murders in three years, and you stopped it."

Irving smiled, "so it bought me points." Still, in his head, was firm disbelief. What he struggled to vocalize was the question of whether or not his subconscious could come up with what was being told to him.

"You got it. It's a technicality more than anything, because murder is still objectively negative. But that guy was a wretch so c'est la vie."

"Okay, I think I understand," Irving said with a few nods.

The mirror image slowed its pace enough to get behind Irving. "Good. Good luck."

"Good luck? Bu—" Irving spun to see he was alone again.

Above him, perched on a tree branch, a sparrow with black eyes began cackling, as if it were a crazed human.

5—Two Miles In

Irving's knees were a train wreck. His mind, worse, like a ratty and darkened sponge.

Even had he not had a full-fledged conversation with himself, he would've been doubting not only his sanity but his ability to make it the rest of the way into town.

He thought of Sara and the kids. Sara, a nurse who worked her fingers to the bone, hardly ever home. But that was far from their marriage's most prominent issue. Irving knew he was a drinker. Knew that it had a tendency to mess up just about every worthwhile thing in his life. The plan, initially, was to part ways once Candace went to college.

They had talked about it for years. It was not to be, as Paul's birth would end up elongating the marriage.

When I get back, Irving thought, *if I get back, I'll set her free. Maybe that's what I'm supposed to do.*

The double-edged sword of it all, staying together for the kids, is that when unhappy married couples stay together for the kids, they're just exposing the kids to a consistently toxic relationship. Toxicity festers and proximity does it no favors.

So, what to do with him in that dynamic?

Yes, that must be the test too, to heal his family via his absence. Leave the money with…the MONEY!

His and Freddie's pitiful $12,000 haul from the bank sat beneath the floorboards of the shack, somewhere below the cot. By now, who knows what had happened to it. He looked down to Guppie and wondered if perhaps his

instinctive choice for Guppie's life over money—not even

thinking of the money until now—would be a positive thing.

A preferable option in the eyes of his delusion.

He hoped it would. He hoped it would be a day of

confirming semi-long held suspicions. That no one truly

was looking for him. That his focus wasn't on the money.

The opposite was true for his newfound suspicion. That,

today, Guppie would die.

6—Eyes Roll Over

With less than a mile to go—and the ground soaking from the rain that now covered the companions—two things were becoming clear. First was that Irving's knees had a few more strides at best. Second was that Guppie was taking his last breaths. When it comes to the health of a man's pet, he just *knows*.

Slowly and pained, Irving lowered Guppie into the sloshy ground below. His fur became caked in mud; grass intertwined with the hair follicles. The dog's stomach gave a few faint movements.

Thump...thump......thump.........thump

The rained picked up and Irving took the moment to wipe the rain, and a tear, from his face. Then, a soft whimper emitted from below, an exasperated puff of air. Guppie's last.

He lay motionless, sinking ever so much further into the mud. Irving put his hands to his face and sobbed.

"Please, God, don't let me be alone out here...please."

He wobbled and sat himself back into the mud. He removed his mud-caked hands from his face, leaving residual grime and the outline of his palms, like a farmer's tan. He placed his hands over his knees and just stared at Guppie.

"I tried to do what was right," Irving stifled back more tears, "I really did."

He placed his hands back over his face. A few specks of mud touched his eyes which he wiped with his forearm, only smearing it across his cheekbones.

He didn't notice a bird swoop down and land on Guppie's body. Not immediately. It was as if it were seizing the moment. It was a blue bird, its beautiful feathers glimmering from the beating sun. So bright, that the reflection caught Irving's attention as he wiped the mud out of his vision.

Their eyes met, and then it was the bird who just stared.

"Hey. Hey, you!" Irving lunged forward and, for the second time in his life, could swear he saw an animal grin. An impossibility. Its beak...curved. The bluebird dodged his swat and swerved through the air, bumping into a falling, dead leaf.

It hovered in the air, preparing to dive towards Irving and Guppie. Then, its eyes rolled over pure black. Unholy, as if this wasn't even a bird. Completely unnatural, it wasn't something that belonged here on Earth. It narrowed its body, holding its wings tightly up against its body for enhanced speed.

As Irving lunged again the bluebird dodged and soared straight into Guppie's open mouth. Irving slid, his knees splashing mud as he tentatively moved his hand towards Guppie's mouth. His hand wavered with little chance of slowing as it inched closer to Guppie's teeth. He could see no bird.

He peered in, cranking his neck for a better angle before he reached into Guppie's mouth, not truly thinking. He just had to get that...monster, from out his friend's mouth.

He barely even registered the events that followed as they progressed.

Guppie's mouth curved upwards, a grin that made Irving wish he himself were dead. It clamped down on his forearm. His teeth pierced Irving's flesh up and down his anchor tattoo. He shook and shook, spraying Irving's blood around. As Irving screamed in pain, Guppie let go, his eyes fully black, still grinning. He backed up a few paces, his movements suddenly robotic.

Irving lay back on the ground, inching away as well. Blood and sinew dripped, nearly poured from the encircling wound on his right arm.

Now fully in shock, Irving shook and sweat. He stared to the sky, taking note of his rapid-pace breathing. He tried to slow it up until he felt pressure from on his legs. There was no slowing it now.

Guppie's right leg climbed atop Irving's left knee, then vice versa as the dog scaled up his owner's shivering body. He walked directly on Irving without fail, as if he were ae tightrope.

Irving held his eyes closed and avoided any sudden movements. "Gup, Gup what are you doing? Please, boy, I just wanted to help ya."

Guppie moved up further, his front paws on Irving's belly now. With a little pressure they pierced flesh, drawing blood.

Irving thrusted his head back into the mud, beneath it hard ground that would normally register as pain all its own. Mud and blood mixed as Guppie moved up further, pushing his paw down on Irving's sternum. Guppie's claws extended, piercing flesh again and further. The dog's grin faded as he opened his mouth and moved his teeth over Irving's throat.

Irving felt instinct in this moment, nothing more. He looked down as far as he could at Guppie's face. With the animal's jaw around his throat there was no recognizing his dog in the soulless eyes. Irving's hands twisted as he held its neck, and the dog fell over. Again, motionless. This time, Irving correctly assumed, it was forever.

The blue bird soared from the dark oral crevice and bashed into Irving's face. Its talons sunk into his nose, eliciting a further winced grunt. Then, the bird plunged his beak towards Irving's left eye, its beak scraping his forehead. It was intercepted by the hand of a raging Irving, who, with a quick snap, broke its neck.

He threw the flying assailant against the closest tree, sending out a single smack sound. Then, he looked to Guppie.

Irving put his head back into the mud and screamed with all the energy he had. For the first time in his life, a feeling he did not get with Freddie, he felt like a murderer.

—

As he pushed up to his feet, more blood oozed from

his arm. The more he used it for leverage against the

ground, the more blood exited the wound.

Irving switched to favor his other hand and stood

fully.

He heard a *flump* sound as something metallic hit the

dirt below. He turned and surveyed his surroundings.

Slowly, he scanned his environment. Then, a glimmer from

below. His flip up lighter, giving off a faint reflection from

the setting sun.

Irving had abstained from cigarettes and booze this

long, and for once was actually glad to see his little keepsake victory reminder. In all actuality, it was more about him not

risking a venture into town.

He bent forward, removed the lighter from the

ground, and held it slowly under his right arm. It was, of

course, quite hot. The wound itself was already searing and

Irving knew he needed a brace or he would bite into his

tongue, potentially severing it.

He looked down, saw Guppie's leg, and thought, *No,*

God no.

Around him were only leaves and thin sticks.

Nothing that could withstand biting pressure.

Just slightly above him, to his right, stood a Maple

that extended as far as he could see. About seven feet in the

air a bare branch protruded. Irving lumbered over to it and

leapt. He told himself it was his general weakness at the

moment that prevented him from reaching it. Grasping the

branch with both hands was, in all actuality, his downfall.

The widening of his arm's wounds as he held onto

the branch sent a tremendous rush of pain into Irving's

brain. He fell back into the mud. Ignoring the most pain

he's ever felt in favor of the most anger he's ever felt, Irving

thrust his left fist down into a mud puddle. Slowly, he

glared up to the bare branch.

With everything inside him, he focused. He ignored

the pain on his forehead, his arm, and now his tailbone as

much as he could. He leapt again, this time grasping the

branch with only his healthy left arm. It held his weight, so

he figured it would withstand biting pressure as well. He

applied some pressure of his own and broke the branch from

its home and fell back to the ground. The mud wasn't

especially thick so it was a hard fall, especially on his right

arm, but it could have been worse.

As he sat, he bit down on the branch and

heard it crack one...two...three...four...five...six times as he

moved the lighter around the circumference of his right arm.

He moved it methodically, slowly cauterizing each inch of

his deep bite wound. His nerve endings were on fire, quite

literally, yet not once did Irving scream. All told, all that

really happened was his jaw smashing through nearly half

of the tree branch.

The wound was now charred, undoubtedly still

bleeding internally. But, now, he focused on it less. He

made a decision to view it as if the pain of the flame

counteracted the pain of the wound itself. Or he was going

into shock, yeah it was probably shock. No matter what,

nothing was more important in that moment than what was ahead. He knew it was time to haul ass.

—

He felt thankful, as he pushed through the woods, that his legs worked. There wasn't just one thing he had to do immediately, there were several. Number one, it appeared this time, had to be business. If what his mirror image said meant anything, the truck should still be at T&M. He didn't plan on driving it though. He figured that would go quite poorly. What he needed was in the cupholder of the center console.

Too much to do at once, it's impossible, one part of him thought.

Focus on the little things you old bastard. One small task, then the next. Step by step, thought another. Irving began counting each step to distract himself.

"Well, I'll be damned if you don't look worse for wear," said the mirror image's voice from behind him again.

"Probably not the best time to use that terminology," it said as it moved before him.

Irving stood rigid, his eyes narrowing. "And where were you," Irving said, "when I needed *you*?"

"Oh, you needed me? That's not how this works. This is for *you* to do. And how about your family? They needed *you* and *you* ran out into the woods like a coward. Don't remember that being a part of the heist plan, Ocean's

336

Eleven." The Mirror Image was fuming, Irving knew that look well enough, but then he saw something he didn't usually see. He saw his face go from furious to collected. "Listen, you've been doing we—" the Mirror Image said as it raised its hands in surrender.

"Just, shut up, you, you liar." Irving's teeth chattered, though not from anger like a cartoon character. His blood loss had been substantial, his mind was weary, and his body the same. "You said I would be okay if I did the right thing. I was doing the right thing and Gup…"

"Yeah, Irv, I never said the dog *wouldn't* die. And, for what it's worth, Buffalo Springfield, I never said you'd live either."

Irving swung at the Mirror Image, who stood still. His fist went right through.

The Mirror Image smirked, "Can't believe that didn't work". He straightened his face and temperament again. "I'm sorry, I'm sorry."

"Leave me alone!" Screamed Irving.

"Look, you're almost there." It pointed through the woods, which were becoming thinner and thinner as far as Irving could see with his weary and diminished vision.

The Mirror Image continued, "You actually aren't doing so bad man. I never said it would be easy. You've gotta win the bronze at least once to appreciate the gold. You did pretty well with the Scouts, after all."

"The Scouts?"

"The birds. They're essentially a watchful eye being held over everybody who narrowly escaped The Reset. See, that'd be you. Everyone, not just people like you has free

will but there's also God's plan to contend with. Free will
and God's plan, it's like a first draft is done but the story's
not *quiiite* written fully just yet."

"The wolf, too."

"Yeah, sure, but the wolf would be a Sentry. That
particular Sentry was watching you from moment one. The
moment you stepped in the woods, you were being watched
muh friend. Every second. Didn't you feel that?"

"Yes, I guess I did."

"Well, Guppie did too. But, see, timing is
everything. Some resolutions we have to arrive at ourselves.
Then, it's all about choice. Things may seem like shit, but
could be worse, you could be dying alone…just the worms."

Irving didn't even realize that he was no longer counting steps. He was just moving, distracted. All around him, the forest grew thinner and thinner.

The mirror image continued, "You, my friend, have hit that three feet below rock bottom place. You can go further one way or hit the road towards the other so make a few positive decisions each day, ones that can only lead to the *betterment* of your existence and keep track."

"Keep track of what? Whether or not my decisions are improving my life?"

"No…others'."

7—Kash

Jon Kash stood in front of his sliding plate glass door with his long arms behind his wide back. As usual, there was a grimace across his irreparably scarred yet futilely botoxed face.

From behind him, a door slammed.

He turned to face two men, mid-thirties, standing in his living room, heavily comprised of a long couch facing two chairs.

"And?" Kash asked impatiently.

The man to the left had blonde hair and his height paled in comparison to his black hair bowl cut buddy.

"Sir, we found the truck." Said Smallblonde in his thick southern accent.

"Yessir and it was locked. We tried to pick it but it ain't so easy with the eighteen-wheelers, ya know," said Tallbowl.

"No, I *don't* know. That's why I hired you two. Because *you* are supposed to know." He turned back to the window. "Wishful thinking it seems."

He reached to a small glass end table next to his maroon couch and took a sip of scotch which he then rubbed from his mustache with his arm. He had yet to offer the two chairs to his guests. "So, where was the truck?"

"Garage of an auto body shop," said Smallblonde. "Right license plate and everything."

"Which auto body shop?" Kash's interest grew even more.

"Uh," Tallbowl chimed in, "T&M's."

Kash sighed with a hint of unexpected anger. "And the owners?"

"We didn't run into anybody but it has been a few months since The Reset so…"

"So, what?!" Kash roared and slammed his hands on the glass coffee table, shattering it and leaving just the frame intact.

The still standing Smallblonde and Tallbowl both gave a reactionary hop.

Smallblonde took over. "The place was dead as could be. Even with taking the intervening months into account it was still readily apparent that The Reset struck

that place pretty hard."

"Okay. And you didn't get into it?"

"The truck?"

"Yes."

"Well, we did, we just had to jimmy it open with a

crowbar."

"That must've been noisy, boys."

"It was, at first. Not many folks around, though.

People just ain't in a shopping mood. No reason to be

around." His deep twang irked Kash.

"Understandable, and did any of these 'not many'

folks see you break into the truck?"

"Nossir, they did not." Smallblonde grumbled very softly. Inadvertent and, thankfully, unheard. Still, he took shit for business, but only up to a point. Boss or not, Kash was cutting it close.

"Not that I can think of," said Tallbowl.

Kash rolled his eyes, still looking out the window. "And the money?"

"No money," replied Tallbowl

"No money? None in the trailer?"

"Trailer?" Tallbowl asked.

"Yes," Kash said more frustrated than ever, "the big shipping container-like thing...you know what—" He turned around and pointed to Tallbowl, "you don't talk anymore." He pointed to the Smallblonde, "you."

345

"Sir," began Smallblonde, "we searched that thing asses to elbows and didn't find a cent. Please forgive us."

"Gents if you want forgiveness you can go searching for the good lord. I expect certain things from you two. Now if those expectations should fail to be met I'm going to move the aim," he pulled a gun from beneath his vest, "of my anger. Now that doesn't sound too good to you, does it?"

Smallblonde and Tallbowl wagged their heads frantically.

Kash smiled. "No, what you'll do is another task…this one unpaid, just like I am, apparently. Think you can handle it?"

"Ah, yessir, what is it?"

"I need you two to look in on the family of an old friend of mine."

Maybe that'll spark a torch under ol' Irving's ass, Kash thought.

8—Last Night

One of the benefits of the shack's location, Irving had

figured, was that it was basically in a valley. Not too far

below the town's elevation. Now it felt like he was moving

up from the summit of a mountain. Exasperated. That was

the word for Irving as he trudged up the final, but largest,

hill en route to the center of town.

"No way to go," he bent over and began coughing.

He held his hand to his mouth before continuing, "but up."

He looked to his palm and found it to be smeared by a

crimson streak.

"Christ, first…", he lumbered over to a tree and slid

back-first down the bark until he was sitting firmly on the

ground. "A rest. Until I can get back on my feet. That's all."

With that, his eyes closed.

Not fully awake, not fully asleep, his mind raced in a near-fugue state. It was like his drinking days. You get piss drunk again to remember memories you've lost from a blackout.

He dreamed of the previous night.

—

About two months ago Irving got the idea his final night in the shack was coming up. Call it premonition, call it boredom, call it remorse, call it what you like. He just *knew*.

Per usual, he adjusted his solar powered radio to local news, which played on near repeat throughout each day so folks could catch up on the town's mundane details.

About nine evenings out of ten he would get a signal, in spite of the shack being below ground level. The news would play until about eight thirty, eight forty-five and then switch to static. This is how Irving slipped into each night.

That evening, though, he could swear he heard the news playing around midnight. Still neither awake nor asleep, his eyes fluttered half open and his auditory senses perked up slowly.

It wasn't until now, though, that the memory changed from forgotten yet absorbed to fully comprehended. It had been some sort of transmission. That should be impossible, but it happened.

But, how?

The voice: "We here at KAB Radio 1330 wish we could tell you all more about what has happened. We truly do not know. Our broadcast tonight, as you may be able to tell, is unlike any other. Don't adjust your station. We live, now, in an unprecedented time. A divided world has become further broken as loved ones…all of us, have lost. We've all lost someone over the past few weeks. Rumor mills circulate, zealots on the streets smirk with self-satisfaction. We may very well be at the end of…all this. All this. Across towns, across cities, people have disappeared right before our eyes. We seem to find no true correlation between those who have disappeared, or amongst those who remain for that matter."

The announcer coughed.

"What we do know, is that all over the world people have vanished, leaving only unremovable marks on the ground in their place. As of now, we do not know if this is due to some form of genetic interference, or if it's sickness, or if there is immunity. What we do know, is that some have gone and some remain. And, now, the question...does this prove...no. I'm sorry, folks, some questions shouldn't be asked. We're going to stick with our usual sign off despite today's circumstances. Good night, sleep tight."

Groggy, Irving questioned the validity of what he heard and with some level of immediacy, fell asleep. From there, he stashed the memory but held the idea.

A few flickers from the radio before, suddenly,

California Dreaming by The Mamas and The Papas rang out

in intermittent segments.

—

Irving awoke to find himself walking. It wasn't the

first time he had done so. This, however, was the first time

he felt grateful it was happening. He typically referred to it

as operating at twenty-five percent, like day three of one of

his binges.

Sitting just between the woods and the town of Westcrick was a church. He came upon it now. It looked like it hadn't been tended to in some time. The gutters were chock full of leaves, a few windows were broken.

Here he was, his feet just at the very end of the forest. Crisp, dying, brown leaves ceased to fall all around him as he reached the clearing. Looking up, no more thickets of bare branches, just a soulless gray sky.

He stopped, and went into the church.

Peering around, he saw no one.

On the walls were written the words, in various places: *Clean Slate.*

Elsewhere: *The Time Is NOW.*

Towards the towering steeple roof: *Going Forward Only LOVE.*

There were several black, dusty marks on the ground. About half of the pews were flipped. There were torn papers, perhaps sheets from a hymnal, floating from the wind he let in. One top of the undisturbed ashy black marks sat soot-covered clothing.

Soot? Irving rubbed his index finger across the ground, allowing some of it to stick to his index finger pad. Upon realizing what it really was, he waved his finger frantically but to no avail. He then rubbed the ash and bone particles on his shirt.

With that, he burst through the church's front doors. Instantly, he fell down the stairs to the ground, and sobbed. In his mind, he prayed, "Be there...please Sara, be there. Be home. Kids, be home. Please. Please, God."

After sitting, rocking his cradled body, for a few minutes, he got up and moved towards Westcrick. While there were not many people, there were a few. All sullen. All walking with their heads to the ground.

See, who give a damn 'bout me? Nobody. World's a whole helluva lot bigger.

He was partially right.

He stopped at the curb on Main Street, looked left and right, no incoming cars either way. Odd, even in a small town like Westcrick there were usually incoming cars on Main Street, for God's sake. Now, nothing.

He moved across the street and peered through the window of Westcrick Drug & Collections, the owner of which was a sort of local renaissance man. He was the town pharmacist and also served as a debt collecting agent. He stayed busy, but was lenient with the residents of Westcrick. Bud Levine was his name. If anyone in town was the notoriously withdrawn Irving's best friend, it would be Bud. How fitting.

He looked in the window for Bud and saw no one. No customers, no Bud, no one. There were five total aisles, each in two parts. However, there was an aisle that had half blocked off with yellow tape and a CAUTION: WET FLOOR sign. Towards the center of it, receiving just enough natural light from the windows to be seen, was another black, dusty mark.

Cobwebs had formed on the store's requisite two by four flat panel lights. Yet, they were on.

Bud's daughter, Letitia, was suddenly behind the pharmaceutical counter. She was looking at Irving, then waving him in with a smile on her face.

Why does this feel like another Mirror Image delusion kind of situation?

Irving passed through the door, knocking the entrance's bell as the door pushed the dangling chain. He never liked it, but it was folksy. Yet another little nuance to make tourists think they had stepped into an episode of *Leave it to Beaver*. He was beginning to feel like it was more *The Twilight Zone* or *The Outer Limits* than anything else.

"Hey, Lee, where's your dad today?"

Letitia stared at him briefly, then said, as if she had not heard the question, "Where have you *been*, Irv?"

"Oh, I—uh—I've been out of town on business." He rubbed the back of his neck. Terrible liar.

"Huh…Irving, dad's dead." Still, a blank stare. As if his question was a stupid one. Coincidentally, that's how he was feeling.

"What happened?"

"It wasn't The Reset…I'm assuming you even know what *that* is." She shot him a confused and skeptical look. Then, her look drooped to pure misery. "He locked himself in the garage, wrapped a bungie cord around the doorknob and a support beam to keep us from getting in, and shot himself in his pickup. After Mom…and since you were gone…" She trailed off.

I guess the Mirror Image was right. "The Reset" …of all the ridiculous reasons to get away with armed robbery.

"Your Mom?"

"The Reset. She started working as a correctional counselor about two months prior. Loved it. Then, one day, she's sitting with an inmate client and…poof. Apparently the guy just sat there with his jaw wide open. It got my husband, too. But, no one's crying over that."

Her husband had a tendency to drink and express his sorrow over his life-long downward trajectory in a physical manner. A real scumbag, Irving always thought. He wasn't wrong.

"My wife?"

"Christ, Irving, where have you been? Really?"

"As I said, away."

Back in the day, Bud would've joined Irving on a job. So, Letitia knew the look of track covering. This much was very apparent from her disbelieving expression.

"Your wife's fine; kids too. You telling me you haven't even been to see them?"

"Going there now."

"Where's your truck, anyway?" Letitia pushed herself up from the counter, peering out the window, looking left and right."

"I'm walking today."

Letitia was done searching for the truth. "Okay, Irving, you're walking today. Would you walk your ass home to see them, then?"

"Yeah, good idea."

"You really seem more out of it than usual, Irv. Ya really do."

"Yeah, can I grab a Tylenol on my way out?"

"Sure."

"I don't have any cash, though, Lee."

"Guess The Reset didn't change *every*thing. You're why I find the argument about whether or not people change...humorous." She smiled to herself for a moment. "Yeah, take a bottle, we only have the generic acetaminophen but you can take one. I think you need it."

"Yeah, thanks Lee."

"You need to find a new line of work, Irv."

Irving said nothing as he swiped one of the few remaining bottles from their section, pulled the front door open, and stepped out.

Next to the shop was a steel green water fountain. The type one would find in a public park. He pushed the button but nothing happened.

"Dry, then", he said as he gulped a pill down. He threw the cotton ball and adhesive tab in a sidewalk trash bin. It toppled right off the overflowing trash. With a sigh, he turned off Main Street, setting off towards home.

Before home, though, there was the police station. It was unavoidable unless he were to circumnavigate the town, but his off-putting conversation with Letitia had put him in a worried hurry.

To the front, he'd be showing himself through the panel glass windows. He chose the back. He slowed his pace, sneaking, as if that would do anything. Then, he stopped fully. Behind the station was a cage for the police dogs. Not only was it big, it was close, sitting next to the chain link fence lining the back portion of the station's property line. He continued in a slow pace before one of the dogs burst out of its house and leapt on the cage, barking and snarling. He knew they did this to everyone but it scared the hell out of him. He burst forward, noticing out of his peripheral an officer move out onto the long, concrete back porch section the officers usually used for smoke breaks when they had desk duty, which was frequently.

"Hey!", the officer yelled as Irving left eyesight.

Irving stopped cold and closed his eyes with a defeated and frustrated wince.

Then, he heard a whistle. "Come on, boy!" Called out the policeman just before another whistle.

Irving got to moving again, but only in a speed walk.

Up ahead was a perpendicular street. He jostled awake his sense of direction. This street, then the two next it, and he'd be home. Part of him wanted to continue in his newfound burst, the other was fearful. What was he even going to say to Sara? "Hi, honey, I'm home. Sorry, I forgot the milk."

Or, could he make up some nonsense about his business trip being delayed because of The Reset, which he still was really sans clue about. It would make partial sense, considering the phone lines seemed to be down. And it's not as if he could ever afford a cell. He'd find a middle ground. He'd come up with something. Either way, he was a terrible liar and his wife was like a wolf hunting a rabbit when it came to spotting bullshit from him.

—

He arrived. It still was what it always was: one of the smaller homes in Westcrick. A rancher with blue shutters, Iving's pride and joy was the relatively small, concrete front porch with a swing attached to the roof. Built it himself. Well, maybe with a little help. All it needed was a literal white picket fence. That was Irving's argument.

They had the opportunity to upgrade their living situation after Sara got her promotion to ICU Nurse Manager a few years back, but they figured the money would be better put to use elsewhere for two reasons. The first was Candace's college fund could use some beefing up. The second was that, due to the size of their hometown, her promotion did not result in a six-figure salary.

It was a matter of necessity, considering the household was essentially fully reliant on Sara's income. As a rule of thumb, she paid her own way and their kids' way. Nothing went to him. He'd just burn it in some dive bar or worse. He was required to assist with utilities as well as stay sober around the kids. The latter he did effectively, for the most part.

He unlocked the gate latch and gently closed it behind him. No sooner did he do that did Sara open the front door. He nervously watched as she pushed the storm door open with her left elbow. It creaked—he never did fix that—but Irving hardly noticed; he was transfixed on her face. A look of awe. A lack of expectancy. Then, a switch to anger.

Irving raised his hands in a white flag gesture. "Hon', hon', I know."

"I would ask where you've been Irving, but it doesn't matter."

Paul rushed out, nudging his mother against the storm door. He gasped as he saw his father's physical condition but continued further anyway.

Irving bent down and picked up Paul, giving him pecking kisses on his cheeks. He flipped him around and carried his giggling son under his arm.

"Lose something?" He asked Sara, before bending in for a kiss. This was not returned as Sara walked back into their dimly lit house. He should have figured.

Sara looked to Paul, "Sweetie, go to your room for a minute, close your door."

"Hard to believe he's five." Irving said with a gently wavering voice as Paul made his way down the hall.

Sara kept her voice low. "Well...you've missed a lot."

Once Paul's door closed with a thud, Sara turned to Irving. "I mourned you. I mourned you and you've been alive this whole time. Thing is, a big part of me already figured that was the case."

"Sara, with all of this plague stuff," Irving said before Sara cut him off.

"Plague? It's not a *plague* Irving, people just," she

raised her arms up in a *whooshing* motion, "disappeared. All

over the world, gone."

She held up a finger and moved into the kitchen. He

heard some pots banging from within the island.

Sara continued from the kitchen, "Now I don't know

if you were off screwing some…*hussy* again, or went on

another bender, but it doesn't matter."

"Sara, I wasn't away because of either of those

things. I wasn't running around, I wasn't…" he peered

down the hall, "fucked up again. I swear. Sober as a bird."

Sara re-entered the room with a first aid kit and her

personal nurse's bag. She bent forward and sniffed him.

"Well, at least you don't reek of booze. You do reek, though.

Good Lord, Irving." She pulled the shirt off of his body,

with it sticking in parts because of dried blood. She removed a puff of cotton from her bag, dabbed it in alcohol and blotted it across his arm. Finally, she unraveled gauze and wrapped it all around.

"That'll stave off infection, at least."

"Have they said what all this is? Are there guesses? I ran into Letitia at the pharmacy, she told me…"

He decided not to mention his conversations with the ghost of Christmas nightmare.

"Bud. Yes, Bud killed himself Irving. No note, but everyone knew why. Once Mel was Reset, then…you. Once he thought you were gone I guess it was too much. Losing a wife and a best friend made everything seem, like I said, too much. I guess."

371

Irving got the feeling she felt something comparable. His heart sank.

They moved into their small living room and sat in opposing furniture, a glass coffee table separating them.

Irving sat in a rocker next to their fire place, Sara on the couch, putting her feet up on the coffee table. Around them were pictures of relatives, a portrait of a lake with a lone fishing boat, and various knickknacks.

Sara bent to her left and picked up a coffee mug from an end table. She looked down in it, flashed a pained look, shrugged, and took a sip. "The media has no clue, people have no clue, and you know what that leads to...biblical talk. Someone pretty high up in the government, can't remember his name exactly, he started the biblical talk. Televangelists caught hold of the notion and spread it because, of course. The people who think it was the legitimate apocalypse, you know…they're saying only the 'good' people are left, yet, still finding a way to have enemies. It was the chief of staff!"

Irving jumped back a bit at her derailment.

She continued, "But a couple days later he got his throat ripped out by a wolf while giving a talk on live TV, so, guess he didn't make the cut."

Irving stared. "You're kidding."

"Nope."

"I think there's something to the wolves, and the birds. When I was out there…"

"Out *where*, Irving?"

"Out in the woods, literally." He waited for her to raise a brow. Her stare remained blank. "Hon'—I guess it doesn't matter now—hon', you know that bank over in Chestshire?"

"That was you?!"

"Please, please, just listen. I don't know if it was hallucination, well I don't think it was now, because I saw, like, a copy of myself."

Immediately, Sara's face soured. She shot him her masterful *you've been drinking* stare. He waved his hands downward several times as if to say *I know, but listen.* "This copy told me about The Reset; used that exact phrase. He also said the birds were 'Scouts' and the wolves 'Sentries'. Do those terms mean anything to you?"

Some of the sourness on her face transformed to surprised belief. "Not really, outside of the natural definitions. But there *have* been bird attacks, too. Real Hitchcock stuff. Honestly, at this point, even after just a month and a half or so, nothing surprises me. As if The Reset wasn't bad enough, mortality rates are...*high*, as in at extreme rates. All the things killing us on top of all the things that were already killing us. It's like ordering dessert at a pizza joint. 'How was your pound of artery clogging garbage, want some more, but different?' People have been scooping up guns left and right and they've been using them. Damn, have they been using them. Everyone feels threatened." She looked off. "Anyway, where exactly *have* you been?"

"The shack."

"You were serious about the woods? You've been in that miniscule, decrepit piece of shit for almost sixty days? How are you alive? Shit, I didn't even know that thing still existed."

"I made due."

"I noticed you don't have Guppie." She said it carefully.

"Guppie saved my life. A wolf."

Sara got up, patted his shoulder, and said as she left the room, "Well, you're gonna have to tell Paul because I'm not doing it. I'm going to bed, Irving. I'm working a twelve to twelve tonight and it'll probably be longer. The hospitals are packed, as I'm sure you can imagine. Tomorrow morning, I can get you in for that wound. Somehow it doesn't appear infected but it will be, I can tell you that much." As she stood on the staircase, she wiped her hand from the top to the bottom of her face, glanced at Irving quickly, and continued up the stairs.

Sara was pragmatic, realistic. Realism and optimism are infrequently the same thing. Initially he loved that about her. Over time it became grating. Now, in all this mess, it seemed to fit like a pesky puzzle piece.

All Irving could think of was more macro scale pondering. Those who remained were questioning whether their loved ones had ascended...or been damned. And, no matter the answer, what did that mean for them? It was too much to mull.

"Okay. G'night, Sara." There was nothing else to say. Nothing he felt would do any good. She seemed accepting, but, just like everyone else, she seemed in a numb daze. Exhausted. Defeated. In that moment he knew no

one was after him for the robbery. It didn't matter. And it

did.

9—Make Peace with the Beast

She hadn't told him to leave yet also hadn't told him he could stay. Irving had moved to the couch, which he figured would be his bed for the foreseeable future anyway, and drifted to sleep.

He awoke to chattering on the TV, "With all this, all this clenching evil upon our society, unseen mostly, we cannot think of ourselves as individuals anymore. Not now, maybe never again. And if that's a hard truth, I apologize. But, if I accepted it, I assume that you can too." The well-dressed newscaster was not reading from a script, no monitor, he was just talking.

"Channel six has gotten real improvisational," Irving said as he rubbed his eyes of their crust and noticed a sticky note barely clinging to the TV.

Leaning in the living room's doorway, with his right foot hooked up and over his left, was the Mirror Image, sipping a cup of coffee.

"Don't say I never did anything for ya."

Irving started rubbing his harm.

"Irving, stop picking at it. Get up, you have work to do," the Mirror Image said as he pointed to the TV.

The Mirror Image approached it as the reporter kept speaking. "We must have patience with our professionals. Our scholars, our doctors…an individual can be brilliant, a crowd can only be insane."

Irving picked the remote up from the coffee table and pressed the power butt a few times. Nothing. He wasn't particularly paying attention to the TV at this point but it appeared it wasn't going to turn off. Was he meant to watch more? Irving's mind anxiously rattled off rhetorical questions.

"The batteries in the remote," said the Mirror Image.

Irving pushed the button of the TV itself and it clicked off. He gave a sarcastic smile to the Mirror Image before picking the note off of it.

Someone who referred to himself as Johnny Cash (?) called. Rude man. Know who he is? Deal with it, please. Bear in mind, if you're still doing your thing, you're out. For Good.   -Sara

"Kash. Shit."

He wrote Sara a note of his own. Amongst the details was the location of the large leather sack beneath the shack.

10—Burn the Bridge

Irving gripped the steering wheel of his Honda Civic so hard he began to worry about calluses. No time to think of such small bananas. It wasn't just his time that was limited now, but his family's. Kash calling the house of someone in his little Family was unprecedented.

It had all been a lie. It was never about the money. What was it about, respect? Irving knew Kash the fencer and Kash the man valued three things: his family, money, and respect. Not all necessarily in that respective order.

He'll think I ratted. But he should know me better. What would I think, though, if I hired someone for a job, it goes to shit, and they disappear? I'd think he's in a holding room with a light

bearing down on his pupils.

I'll stroke his ego. Lord knows he likes that, but it won't be

enough. I can't prove to not have what I don't have. It's my word

against Freddie's and Fred's dead. Doesn't look so good. But I'll

give him the diamonds. Whether or not I live through this, which

is looking laughable, at least they'll be set up financially. That's

better than they've had it.

Jonathan Fletcher Kash had a house in the

mountains. Gorgeous, mid-century modern with

renovations seemingly every other month. To look at it was

to see the home of a man for whom nothing obviously was

ever good enough; never complete. Irving prayed that that

portion of his psyche would subside when they met. The

hope that longevity of acquaintance would supersede

distrust.

Irving knocked on the door, peered right through the open-faced façade, and saw no one. Because of this, his nerves, or a combination of the two he jumped when Kash himself suddenly opened the door. Usually, he had one of a revolving door of hired help do this. Not today.

Kash said nothing and held nothing. He pushed his right palm onto Irving's breastbone and rubbed down to his belly as his left-hand braced Irving's shoulder to keep him from falling backwards. Or perhaps running. Either way it was a half-hearted attempt at a hug.

"No wire, Jon."

Kash jerked his head, inviting Irving in.

"Sit down." He said coldly. "Did you know Kentucky Fried Chicken is like a Christmas tradition in

385

Japan? People dress like the colonel, even. With your beard and mustache, that's what you remind me of. The colonel."

Irving smirked, despite knowing he was being made fun of, and looked around Kash's home.

Amongst the many lavish accoutrements were some out of place deer skulls hanging from the wall. A grotesque display of power, as far as Irving was concerned.

Beneath one such skull sat a bar, which Kash moved to and began pouring a glass of bourbon. He stuck it out to Irving, who waved it off as he sat on Kash's burgundy velvet couch.

"You give it up for good this time?" Irving couldn't tell for sure whether Kash was being sincere or condescending.

"I wasn't drunk on the job either, Jon. Swear to God."

"Weird time to swear to God. God hasn't seemed to care about folks recently."

"Jon, I just learned about this whole thing. Trust me, I know less about it than you. But a merit-based apocalypse? Jon?" Irving shook his head.

"You 'just learned about this whole thing'." Kash leaned back against the bar. He stirred his massive daiquiri. "All the time you were gone I was thinking, 'The longer he's in there the more he's gonna start shaking and I don't want to see what happens when his loose change falls out.' You needed some plausible deniability and I gave you it."

He took a very long sip of his drink. Irving got a brain freeze just from empathy. "Did you know that I had a niece?" Kash asked with some energy.

"Uh, no. Was she taken in this Reset thing?"

"No, y'all beat it to the punch."

"Pardon?"

"See, I know you don't kill." He began walking towards Irving, waving his hands, "You're very 'though shalt not kill', which I've always respected, mind you." Kash let the moment land. "Freddie, though, *ooh* Freddie. He had a real taste for it."

"I noticed." Irving's tone took a trip to the arctic.

"Yeah, noticed so hard you broke your little rule, didn't ya?"

"He crossed a line."

"And you didn't? No, what Freddie—the *boy*—did was his job. If anyone fucked up—" he took a sip of his drink, pointing at Irving with his pinky. "That'd be you, slick."

"So, this is about Freddie. Not the money?"

"Why would I have you rob a bank just one town over, Irv? Why? Did that make sense to you even at the time? Much less now, a few months being, well, where*ver* you've been."

"It seemed hinky, sure, but desperate times—"

"Still require orders from your boss to rub out a coworker!" Kash roared and Irving froze. "I...hate...when the car gets off the track. Hate it. Hate complications. You, Irving, are a complication."

"Why were we there, Jon?" Irving's tone betrayed him. It was clear at least part of him already knew.

Kash sat down on one of the ottoman chairs across a coffee table from the couch. "I loved my niece. But she saw something she shouldn't have seen and heard something she shouldn't have heard. Now, she was no narc, no one in my family is. But her cutesy little dipshit boyfriend sure was looking at some charges. Embezzlement, laundering, I dunno, just about everything. Man, I'm telling you, she blew through every paycheck she got hiring the best lawyer. But, let's face it, in a small town...a bank doesn't pay much. Lot of greed out there, it seems." Kash said nothing for a few moments. "This is the part where you give me the diamonds and call me a hypocrite."

"You had Freddie kill your own niece."

390

"Well, *I* wasn't going to do it. I just bent the world to fit *my* will."

Irving had always known Kash to have a temper and a screw that was wriggling loose, but this still seemed out of character. He quickly handed over the small leather sack with diamonds.

"What did she see?"

"Why do you want to know?"

"Fair enough. What can I do to make this right, Kash? You calling my house, that's no good man. Sara's asking questions."

"Let her ask."

"That doesn't help."

"Would it help if I put in a personal appearance?" He crossed his legs one over the other. "Assuage her worries a bit?" He clearly had fun saying the word "assuage".

"No, that would not. A fact of which I'm sure you are well aware. Now, look, I'm not the brightest bulb of the bunch, but there's something…"

"We'll start with fifty K. That's for me to not adopt your little Paul after I handle you and Sara. Irving, see, on the latter part, some things are inevitable. I hate to say, Paul's adoption would be short lived."

"Stay away from my kids. I've known you a long time man, we've worked well together, but you're crossing a fuckin' line."

Kash spoke undeterred. "Kids, plural. Oh, that's right, your oldest. See I've had a few of my boys tailing your little posse for quite some time now. It seems two of them have taken quite a liking to Candace. They call her Candy." He grabbed the straw and slurped from his drink, all the while keeping eye contact with Irving.

Irving rose from the couch.

Kash held up the index finger of his right hand as he bent over and put his drink on the coffee table with his left. He picked up a gray rectangular object, which, up until now, Irving had thought was some gaudy contemporary art centerpiece. Size-wise it could have previously served as the box of a necklace. He flipped it over once. The side that had been facing Kash had, amongst many others, a light blue button right in the center.

"You like it? It's a call button. Exact one they have in the hospitals across the country. They go out of style, bring in the new ones, you can buy these cheap. See, my boys outside, they get a nice little beep when I need them. If you're thinking something along the lines of 'Kash won't kill me, not in his own house,' know that you are right. But Clyde, my bigger boy, a new hire, the difference is he'll actually do it, so *sit down*. Remember, it's not just your life on the table now. Sit...now. Please."

"You had my wife *followed*? My kids? What, you thought I was just hanging around?"

"Oh, as far as you being around was concerned, that ship sailed so long ago I couldn't even see the damn thing. I just knew you were the stubborn type. Might slip a letter or two to your wife to let her know where the payday is."

Irving went cold. *Could he know about the letter I put up before I left?*

But Kash continued, "You are the type that needs a little reminder of who they serve and why they serve. Irving, I have known you for quite a long time. Our lives have taken us some bizarre places, my face can testify to that." Irving watched Kash wait for a response. Presumably so he could reply with a bullet. "All these years, *one* thing has never changed for us. You are, were, and always shall be, a loser. I'm not, plain and simple."

Irving's blood began to boil. "You want *me*. Look, you'll get what you deserve, okay? Anyway, I've just decided that I can love and support my children from a distance. Far distance...as it may be."

Irving lunged up and tripped on the coffee table between the two of them, but he still got a fist on Kash's left cheek bone. With a *smack* ringing out, he adjusted his knee and slipped it almost all the way out of the destroyed coffee table. He kicked forward, hard, and a table leg broke free. Irving grabbed it and swung. As it crunched one of Kash's ribs, Irving felt a sharp pain echo throughout his knee. Broken, at least sprained. The accent chair flipped backwards, sending the two tumbling to the floor, rolling.

Everything moved very, very quickly. Irving continued the struggle, though, as he gripped Kash's throat.

Responding to the call button, Smallblonde and Tallbowl—Christian name Clyde, apparently—stumbled through the sliding pane glass door. They raised their H&K MP7 A1s.

"Get off 'im! Now!" Smallblonde.

Irving made as if he was going to release Kash and back away.

They apparently thought he would do just that. They sent a stream of lead rippling through the moist mountain air to meet him.

Irving pulled Kash up, though, as he fell backwards. Bullets tore through his suit and dress shirt, spraying blood and bits of blue fabric on Irving's face. With that, he himself felt pain.

Kash lay on top of him, dead. Irving slid his hand between the two of them and felt an unbelievably sharp sting. He brought his hand out to see blood rolling down. He was used to the sight of blood, having been wounded plenty of times in the woods, but this was a highly concerning amount.

As he lay his head back, accepting his fate, his gaze moved to the still-open plate glass door. Two wolves entered, looked down to him in unison, and then up to the backs of Smallblonde and Tallbowl.

As Irving's sight faded, entering death, all he heard was flesh tearing, screams, then gurgles.

"You did it." All of a sudden, the Mirror Image was sitting on the couch, eating a pear. "Some people spend a pretty big chunk of their life fixating on their own mortality. They dream in fear of death."

Irving grumbled, not wanting another lecture at the moment.

"Ironic," the Mirror Image continued, clearly waiting for an invitation to further explain.

Instead, Irving responded with: "All sleep is, is a tiny step towards death. Time isn't going to wait. Time doesn't wait, not usually.

The Mirror Image nodded. "Any last questions for the world?"

"Does," Irving groaned, "does time heal all wounds?"

The Mirror Image looked down to Irving's wound, then adjusted his gaze back up to eye contact with a look of trepidation. Some news you just don't want to deliver.

Irving continued, "Not this one. I deserve this and nothing else, *that's* the reality."

"Irving, in the end, people know how you feel about them."

Irving didn't respond vocally. Instead, he closed his

eyes and thought—or rather recognized—*This was my reason.*

This was my fate. This was how they can have a clean slate. Now

take me home.

Made in the USA
Middletown, DE
17 March 2021